Katherine sw

'I have to be marr[...] day.'

'What? But that's only two weeks away!' Damon exclaimed. 'It's impossible for you to meet someone, get to know them and get married in that space of time.'

'That's why I need to ask you to do me a favour. I know it's not what either of us wants but...' She forced herself to meet the deep blue of his eyes. 'Damon, will you marry me?'

Josie Metcalfe lives in Cornwall now with her long-suffering husband, four children and two horses, but, as an army brat frequently on the move, books became the only friends who came with her wherever she went. Now that she writes them herself she is making new friends, and hates saying goodbye at the end of a book—but there are always more characters in her head clamouring for attention until she can't wait to tell their stories.

Recent titles by the same author:

A MILLENNIUM MIRACLE
TAKE TWO BABIES...
A TRUSTWORTHY MAN
BE MY MUMMY
INSTANT FATHER CHRISTMAS

COURTING
DR CADE

BY
JOSIE METCALFE

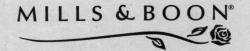

First published in Great Britain 2000
Harlequin Mills & Boon Limited,
Eton House, 18-24 Paradise Road, Richmond, Surrey TW9 1SR

© Josie Metcalfe 2000

ISBN 0 263 81945 0

Set in Times Roman 10½ on 12 pt.
03-0002-49583

Printed and bound in Spain
by Litografia Rosés S.A., Barcelona

CHAPTER ONE

'WILL you marry me?'

Katherine's words echoed hollowly around the cramped room as she grimaced at herself in the mirror. She shook her head.

'This is impossible. I must be mad!'

How on earth did men get up the courage to do it?

The sudden sound of voices outside her door made her jump and she reached hurriedly for her dress as several sets of knuckles beat a simultaneous tattoo on her door.

'Come in,' she called, and a chattering, laughing group almost seemed to explode into her room.

One half of her was relieved at the intrusion. She certainly wasn't doing her nerves any good as she went over and over her crazy plan.

'Aren't you ready yet?' demanded Shari, as stunning as ever in a slinky turquoise dress that looked as if it had been poured over her. 'What are you wearing? Not your basic black again!' She whisked the garment out of Katherine's hands and held it up at arm's length.

'Hey! Now this is more like it!' she exclaimed. 'Glamorous. Where did you find it?'

Katherine thought about the little boutique that she'd haunted while she'd tried to summon up the courage to buy the seductive scrap of nothing. In the dark of a long sleepless night she'd decided to invite Damon out for a meal and had even planned to wear the blue silk dress he'd liked so much at Christmas while she asked for his help. Then she'd remembered an earlier conversation with her grandmother about leap year's superstitions and remembered the hospital's Valentine's ball.

It was only the thought of what she was going to have to achieve while wearing the sexy dress that had propelled her through the door of the boutique. She was going to need every bit of help she could get.

'I thought it was time for a change,' she admitted as she retrieved the dress. Like her old faithful it was black, but that was where the similarities ended. This one managed to combine flirtatious elegance with an indefinable air of mystery as the clever cut hinted at the figure usually kept hidden under the tunic top of her uniform.

Now that she was putting it on it didn't seem to be much longer than her tunic either, and as she was wearing it with sheer black stockings and strappy high heels, rather than uniform trousers, she felt more than half-naked.

As Fran pulled the zip up for her Shari gestured for Katherine to turn round so they could admire the full effect.

'*Very* nice,' Louise said without a hint of envy, her own cuddly curves very different from Katherine's slender figure. 'What's his name?'

'What do you mean?' Katherine's hands were trembling as she tried to fasten the chain of her locket around her throat. 'Who?'

'Well…new dress, new hairstyle. It's obvious there must be a new man,' Fran said avidly, her dark eyes gleaming. 'Is he picking you up here? Will we get a chance to meet him?'

'Sorry.' She shook her head, keeping her eyes on the

reflection of her own pale face in the mirror. 'New dress and new hairstyle but no new man. I'm meeting up with Damon when we get there.'

'Again? But you've just spent all day working with him. You're *not* going to spend the whole night talking shop!' Shari exclaimed.

'Oh, I might just twist his arm into dancing with me once or twice,' Katherine said, her stomach twisting itself into knots at the thought of what else she was going to be asking him to do...if she ever found the courage.

'Well! What a waste!' Louise declared in disgust. 'It's the leap year's Valentine's ball and you're absolutely dressed to kill, and you're settling for a pipe-and-slippers sort of evening while the rest of us are out to have fun.'

'I'd be staying home if I were going to have a pipe-and-slippers evening so, even though I might spend most of the evening talking shop, at least I'm making the effort,' Katherine pointed out as she contemplated covering the dress under her coat. It was February, for heaven's sake, and she was walking round in something with all the substance of a nightdress.

'That's what makes it such a waste,' Shari exclaimed. 'You know as well as I do that after two years there are absolutely no sparks between you and Damon. You look stunning and you should be on the lookout for someone new...someone special. After all, this is the day when *we're* entitled to do the proposing if we find someone we want.'

Katherine's stomach gave another convulsive leap but before she could respond to Shari's friendly nagging there was another rap at the door.

'Are you women ready yet?' demanded a male voice

from the other side. 'If not, we could go and find ourselves a drink while we wait.'

'Don't you dare!' Louise said warningly as she opened the door. 'We're ready and waiting and raring to go. It only happens once every four years and we're going to take full advantage of it. Tonight it's leap year Valentine's day, and it's our turn to do the asking.'

'What?' Steve, her escort for the last three or four months, took a hasty step back. When he'd caught sight of them in all their finery his smile had widened in approval but it was fading rapidly now.

'Don't you remember? Tonight it's us women who get to do the choosing,' Louise gloated. 'We'll be able to go up to any man we fancy and ask him for a dance.'

'And if you turn us down you have to pay a forfeit to swell the hospital coffers,' Fran added.

Steve looked glum. 'Whose bright idea was this? It sounds like feminism gone mad. Is it just because we've reached the twenty-first century?'

'Not at all,' Katherine said, her recently acquired knowledge about the superstitions surrounding leap year and Valentine's Day burning holes in her head. 'Apparently, the custom dates back to the thirteenth century, only in *those* days the woman could actually propose marriage.'

'And the poor bloke had to pay a fine if he turned her down?' Dave, his SHO colleague from Orthopaedics and Fran's escort, was clearly aghast.

'That's right. So you can think yourselves lucky that it's only for one evening and you're only being asked for a dance. In days gone by you'd have had to hide for a whole year if you wanted to avoid the penalty,' Katherine pointed out, trying to ignore the weight of guilt pressing down on her mind as she ushered them out into the corridor. 'I take it the taxi's waiting?'

'Tarik's waiting in it down at the main entrance,' Dave confirmed. 'If he'd come up with us someone might have grabbed it.'

'Has everyone got their tickets?' Fran asked, born organiser that she was. 'We don't want anyone being turned away at the door, not when this could be the night we meet the man of our dreams.'

'Down boy,' Damon murmured to himself when he caught his first glimpse of Katherine.

It had only taken that first glimpse to tell him that she'd pulled out all the stops this evening. That dress should have been declared a hazard to health, especially for the length of leg it revealed.

Why had she donned such a stunning outfit? Had she decided to take advantage of tonight's special theme to find herself a partner with potential for a long-term relationship?

In spite of the fact that the idea of losing their close friendship caused a strange ache around his heart, he couldn't really blame her. She was a beautiful, intelligent woman who deserved to have a man love her enough to make a permanent commitment.

At least he could console himself with the thought that he'd never led her on to expect anything like that from him. All he had to offer was friendship and it was hers for as long as she wanted it.

'Mmm. Nice!' said a husky voice behind Katherine and she turned to face Damon Cade.

'Thank you. You don't look too bad yourself, Dr

Cade,' she said with a mock curtsey, hoping he couldn't see that her smile was a little bit forced.

It was blatant understatement, of course. Most men managed to look good in formal evening wear, but Damon's dark good looks put him in a class of his own.

She'd thought so from the first moment she'd met him when she'd joined the staff on Windermere Ward, but it hadn't taken her long to find out that the attraction only went one way. Since then they'd forged a firm friendship that she valued highly.

It was that friendship that she risked destroying if she ever got the courage to take advantage of tonight's special occasion.

'Problems getting away?' she asked, knowing that he'd been late arriving at the hotel. The easy conversation and relaxed atmosphere between them would be a grievous loss if she ruined their camaraderie.

'Just the usual—a minor riot on Windy,' he said with an offhand grin.

'A riot? I bet Frank was cheating on his computer scores.'

'How did you guess?'

'What else would it be with that group of monsters? Sometimes I think it was a big mistake, putting all the teenagers in together. They don't have to tone things down so much when they're all about the same age.'

'You don't mean that,' Damon chided. 'You know what it was like when they were surrounded by puppies and kittens and Mickey Mouse.'

'They certainly seem to respond to the more adult surroundings on Windy. They seem less likely to bottle their problems up when they're surrounded by their peers.'

Windermere Ward was the relatively new department that had been opened specifically to cater for the special needs of their adolescent patients. Needless to say, it had instantly been renamed Windy's, a fact that the less couth of their charges tried to prove as loudly as possible.

'Have you done any circulating yet?' Damon asked, his lazy grin having its usual unsettling effect on her equilibrium. 'I hope you've done your bit to swell the hospital's coffers.'

'I was waiting for you to arrive,' she said with a wicked smile of her own. 'Are you going to turn me down if I ask you to dance?'

'Certainly not! My Scottish ancestors would turn over in their collective graves if they thought I was paying out good money just to stay off the dance floor.'

He grabbed her hand and began to drag her along behind him like a reluctant puppy.

'Hey, slow down!' she squeaked. 'I can't keep up with your long legs in these shoes.'

He turned to look down at the offending articles and she felt the way his eyes travelled up the length of her scantily clad legs as though he were stroking her.

'They look nearly as long as mine when you're dressed like that,' he said, his blue eyes darker than ever when they finally met hers. 'Want me to carry you?'

Her heart leapt the way it always did when he teased her like this and she had to force herself not to imagine how it would feel to be cradled against him, surrounded by the strength of his arms.

'That won't be necessary,' she said quellingly, but she might as well not have bothered. Her stern expression didn't have the same effect on him that it did on their young patients.

They reached the area of polished wood reserved for dancing, and in spite of the bouncy rhythm of the current tune he turned to wrap his arms around her.

'What *are* you doing?' she demanded as he held her head against his shoulder with one lean hand. He was a toucher—a person who reached out to others without realising he was doing it—but this felt deliberate.

'Claws away, Kat. If we dance like this none of those ravenous women will want to butt in,' he murmured with a chuckle, his breath warming the side of her face and sending a familiar shiver down her spine.

'Coward,' she muttered, and felt him chuckle again as he tightened his arms around her.

'Not at all,' he retorted, his lips brushing over her ear as if he were whispering sweet nothings. 'It's simple self-preservation. I don't want to dance with them and don't want to have to pay for the solitude. I identified the problem and, having formulated a solution, put it into immediate effect.'

Katherine had to chuckle at his audacity but his words struck a chord with her.

She, too, had identified a problem and formulated a solution. The only trouble was, she wasn't quite so courageous about putting it into immediate effect.

She sighed and shook her head, only then noticing that Damon must have stopped off on his way here to change his clothes. His shirt was freshly laundered and smooth against her cheek and she could smell the slightly soapy fragrance that told her he'd recently taken a shower.

She drew in a surreptitious deep breath, knowing that she would recognise him blindfolded just from the scent of his skin.

For two years she'd been storing up myriad useless

facts about the man, knowing that they were all she would ever possess of him.

It had been the first or second day after they'd met...within the first week at least...that they'd found themselves waiting for news from Theatre about a critical patient.

'He's still on the table,' Damon had reported as he'd put the phone back in its cradle.

'Poor kid,' Katherine had murmured as she'd poured boiling water over coffee granules in the bottom of two cups. 'First he's knocked off his bike while playing the fool, then he has an adverse drugs reaction, then his blood pressure plummets because they missed a torn blood vessel.' It had been her sharp eyes that had picked up the signals as she'd done his first set of observations when he'd reached the ward.

'Let's drink this out on the top of the fire escape,' Damon had suggested, grimacing at the noxious evidence that this was the only room in which staff had still been allowed to smoke. 'I've never got used to breathing air I can see.'

Over their cups of coffee in the hush of the early morning they started talking, eventually exchanging tentative snippets of personal information—where they'd trained, what had prompted them to choose this job in this hospital.

'Married?' she asked when they'd reached the subject of families, fully expecting him to say yes.

'Not in this lifetime,' he replied softly, but she'd heard the pain in his voice and wondered what fires he'd been through to make him so adamant.

She subsequently learned about the devastation he'd suffered time and again as, one by one, his family had been taken away from him.

'I was just eighteen and in my last year at school when my little sister got acute myeloid leukaemia,' he said suddenly into the darkness. There was a long pause and Katherine began to think he wasn't going to say any more. She wanted to know but was very certain that he was far too private a person to respond to direct questioning.

'Jessica was a fighter,' he continued eventually. Katherine was watching him and saw just the edge of an admiring smile touch his sombre mouth. 'It looked as though she had beaten it and the prognosis was good when her Hickman line had to be replaced. Something went wrong in Theatre and her heart was damaged. She arrested on the table and they couldn't get her heart started again.'

'Oh, Damon,' she breathed, wishing she knew him well enough to offer him the consolation of a hug. He seemed so very alone.

'Dad had a massive stroke shortly after and just didn't seem to want to fight, and when he went it just took the stuffing out of Mum. I never knew she'd had heart problems for years until I saw her death certificate.'

'How old were you?' Katherine asked softly, unable to conceive how it must have felt to lose so much of his family in such a short space of time. Her own family life had been full of stress as long as she could remember but at least she'd always known her grandmother loved her.

'Damian and I had left school. I'd started my medical training and he'd gone into the army.'

'Damian?' She was so relieved to know that at least he had one member of his family left.

'My twin. Damon and Damian, the demon duo,' he said with wry self-mockery.

'Is he still in the army?'

'He probably would have been if he hadn't gone out to the Gulf,' he said, his voice noticeably thicker. 'I think the army is still trying to kid everyone that there's no such thing as Gulf War syndrome. All I know is that my brother went out there a fit, healthy man and within months of coming back was a physical wreck, hardly able even to lift a cup of tea to his lips.'

The bitterness was almost visible in the air around him and she had to squeeze her eyes tightly shut to stop the tears of sympathy falling.

'I took some leave and went to stay with him to try to get him back on his feet, but it was hopeless. The chemicals had done far too much neurological damage and he was growing worse almost daily—almost as if he was disintegrating from the inside. In the end he couldn't stand the humiliation any longer and took a massive overdose.'

Before she could find any words they were startled by a sharp tap on the window set into the door behind them.

After their harrowing conversation it seemed grimly apt when they were informed that their young patient hadn't survived the emergency surgery.

Unfortunately, knowing in graphic detail the reasons Damon was determined to remain alone hadn't stopped the attraction she felt for him from growing with each passing day.

If it hadn't been for the deep friendship that had been growing between them at the same time she didn't know if she could have borne working so closely with him.

And now she risked destroying it all.

But if she didn't take the risk, there would be another devastating price to pay. Whichever way she looked, all she could see was yet another tightrope, stretching into the distance.

And here she was, swaying gently in his arms, selfishly allowing her emotional needs to postpone what had to be done.

'Damon?' she murmured, shakily deciding that she couldn't delay any longer. Who knew when another member of staff might decide to take advantage of the event to approach him for a dance?

'Mmm?' He sounded half-asleep, almost as lazily contented as a cat in front of a fire, with his cheek resting on the top of her head and his arms wrapped around her as though they belonged there.

'I need to ask you something…a favour.' It wasn't the right word but with her brain so scrambled by apprehension she couldn't think of any other one that fitted the circumstances.

'Well, as we're already dancing I can't be fined for refusing you so I should be quite safe if I agree. What do you want me to do?'

A more energetic dancer jostled into the two of them, suddenly making her realise that anyone nearby could overhear what she wanted to say.

'Um, could we go somewhere a little quieter?' Silently she cursed herself for a coward but it made sense to delay another couple of minutes while they searched out some privacy. She certainly didn't want the whole hospital to know what was going on. If they knew the real story behind her request that would defeat the whole purpose of it.

Besides, she knew it was going to be a shock to him,

and if he refused her out of hand it would be a big enough disappointment, without the rest of the world watching her rejection.

Damon led her through the chattering, laughing throng, batting away a small forest of heart-shaped balloons with his free hand on their way back towards the reception area.

'Is this quiet enough?' he asked with a trace of a frown pleating his forehead. 'Everyone seems to have arrived and made their way through to the other room so we should have some peace here.'

The hotel foyer was spacious and elegant, the marble threshold giving way to deeply carpeted luxury that seemed to absorb any sounds around them.

'It's fine,' she said distractedly, and made towards a rather formal-looking settee overshadowed by an impossibly green palm tree and sank onto it before her knees refused to support her any longer. If only the room weren't quite so brightly lit perhaps she would actually manage to find the words she needed.

'Right, now,' he began as he sat down beside her and automatically took her hand to cradle it between his. 'What's wrong, little Kat? What favour do you need from me that demands this much secrecy?'

There was such concern in Damon's eyes that it warmed her heart but she still didn't know where to start.

'Is it a problem at work?' he prompted. 'You know I'll do anything I can to help you sort it out.'

She shook her head swiftly. 'No. It's nothing to do with the hospital.' It would have been easier to deal with if it had been.

'OK,' he continued almost without a pause. 'A problem with finances, then? Nurses have never been paid what they deserve. I know you'd never let me give you any money—you've got far too much pride for your own good—but I'd willingly make you a loan. Just tell me how much.'

'It's not money,' she said quickly. 'My grandmother set up a small trust for me years ago and it's still sitting there in case I need it.'

'Knowing you and the aforementioned pride of yours, you've made it a point of honour that you won't touch it,' he teased, and she couldn't deny it. She'd always believed in working for the things she wanted…

She grimaced as the realisation struck her that she was about to ask Damon for something she certainly hadn't earned. She wouldn't be able to blame him if he turned her down flat.

'If it isn't the job and it isn't finances then it must be something to do with your family,' he said logically. 'Is it your grandmother? Is she ill? Do you need the names of some specialists?'

'Yes… No…' She shook her head and pulled a face. 'Yes, it's something to do with my family but, no, my grandmother isn't ill. It's… Oh, Damon, I don't know where to start.'

'How about the beginning?' he suggested as he settled himself more comfortably against the back of the settee and pulled her closer, one arm circling her shoulders to tilt her against the solid warmth of his chest. 'Here, settle your head on my shoulder and take your time.'

His patience and kindness were almost her undoing and she only just managed to control the hot press of tears. What would she do if she managed to destroy this precious friendship?

'So,' he began, 'it's about your grandmother and she's in good health. You were worried about her when your grandfather died back in the autumn, but each time you've visited you seemed quite happy with what you found, especially when your mother moved in with her.'

'I was worried, but you're right—with Mum's help she's coped wonderfully. I wouldn't have believed how well the two of them get on after all these years of feuding with Grandfather.'

She'd told Damon long ago that her mother had divorced her father for adultery when Katherine was small. Damon had shared her anger when she'd told him that her mother had been blamed by her father-in-law for being the cause of the first divorce the family had ever known, and had been summarily cut off.

'After my grandfather died, Grandmother told Mother that the house was too big for her to rattle around in on her own. Anyway, I think she's always secretly missed having another woman to talk to.'

'So what's the problem now? You visited them this weekend, didn't you?'

She nodded. 'Saturday and Sunday and back on duty this morning.'

'Obviously one of them said something to you over the weekend.'

'Not directly,' she admitted. 'It was something I overheard. Something they didn't want me to know.'

'About?'

'About my grandfather's will.'

'Uh-oh. I reckon that there are more feuds started over wills than any other legal document. What did he do—leave everything to the local cat shelter?'

'It would have been easier if he had. At least my

grandmother would have had a legal right to stay in the property until her own death.'

'So?'

'Oh, I'm sorry, Damon, it must feel as if you're having to drag the whole thing out of me a word at a time, but I'm still trying to come to terms with it myself. My grandmother has lived in that house ever since the two of them married. That's nearly fifty years so it's not just a house…it's her home. I honestly believed that she and my mother would be able to stay there as long as they liked. Now, because of my grandfather's will, it looks as if it will have to be sold and they'll have to move elsewhere.'

'For God's sake, why? You've always said how much your grandmother loves that house. Didn't he realise that? Didn't he realise that at her age such an upheaval could kill her?'

'I know,' she whispered, shaken to the core by the thought that she might lose her precious grandmother. 'And I know from what I overheard that she's terribly worried about it, but even though I tried to drop hints she just won't talk to me about it.'

'So exactly how did you find out the details? Did you manage to see a copy of the will when you were there?'

'I looked for it before I left to come back to work early this morning but they must have put it away somewhere. All I really know for certain is what I overheard the two of them discussing last night when they thought I'd gone upstairs to have a bath. Apparently, Grandfather was worried that Grandmother wouldn't be able to cope with such a big property and he was afraid that if she was living alone she might have a fall and be unable to call for help.'

Damon was silent for a moment and she angled her head to look up at him in time to see his grudging nod.

'He's got a point, you know,' he said slowly. 'I know she's got your mother living with her now, but he wasn't to know that would happen. Not if he'd been keeping up a feud with her for the last twenty-something years. Is there no way your grandmother can challenge the will on those grounds?'

'Apparently not. He's put in a specific clause—a condition that has to be fulfilled—and that's the only grounds on which she can keep the house and live there as long as she likes.'

The moment of truth was approaching and her pulse was beginning to race as apprehension mounted.

'So, what does she have to do to fulfil the condition? Is it something totally impossible?'

'It's not something *she* has to do, it's something *I* have to do or she'll lose her home.'

'*You?* But…'

'I think it's partly because Mum divorced Dad and then Dad was killed so soon after that. There was no second chance for a male heir to be born.'

'So what does he want you to do—have a sex-change operation to satisfy the will? I can tell you, you're far too pretty to convince anyone.'

That surprised a chuckle out of her.

'Idiot,' she said, and nudged his ribs with her elbow. 'He was far too old-fashioned to have thought of that. He would have hated the very idea.'

'So?'

'I have to get married,' she said bluntly, and held her breath while she listened to the silence stretch out for what seemed like for ever.

It must have been her imagination but Damon

seemed to grow very still except for the brief tightening of his arm around her shoulders.

It seemed light years until he spoke.

'Did he specify a groom while he was about it?' he asked quietly, and she shook her head.

'He was kind enough to make it my choice,' she said acerbically, 'although what I would have been able to do about it if the will had been found any later, or if I hadn't overheard the two of them talking about it, I don't know.'

'What do you mean?' He'd obviously lost the thread for a moment.

'The will had apparently been misplaced and was only found a few days ago, and the two of them weren't going to tell me anything about it. They still don't know that I overheard them worrying about it.'

'So what was that about finding the will in time? I take it he specified a qualifying date to his condition?'

Katherine swallowed hard and nodded, hoping he couldn't tell how tense she was.

'I have to be married by the end of leap year's day.'

'What? But that's only two weeks away!' he exclaimed. 'It's impossible for you to meet someone, get to know them and get married in that space of time.'

'Two weeks and one day, to be exact,' she said, conscious of the tremor in her voice but unable to do anything about it. 'That's why I need to ask you to do me a favour. I know it's not what either of us wants but...'

Knowing it was now or never, Katherine swallowed and snatched a quick breath, nerves sticking her tongue to the roof of her mouth. It was Valentine's Day in a leap year but she'd never thought it was going to be this hard to say the words.

Finally she forced herself to meet the deep blue of his eyes. 'Damon, will you marry me?'

CHAPTER TWO

'ME? MARRY?'

Suddenly there was a foot of artificially heated air between them but all Katherine could feel was the chill where his arm had been.

'I know you told me you never wanted to get married,' she said, hurrying into speech before Damon could refuse her outright. 'But this would be different. It wouldn't have to be a *real* marriage.'

She saw his dark eyebrows draw into a swift frown and hastened to explain.

'I would only need to be married for long enough to satisfy the conditions of the will. As soon as I'd made certain that my mother and grandmother could keep their home as long as they wanted, we could get the marriage annulled.'

He was silent for several very long seconds.

'Is this what your grandmother wants you to do?' he demanded with an unexpected edge to his tone. 'Did she suggest you go out and find someone to proposition just so she can stay in her house?'

'Good God, no! She'd be horrified!' she exclaimed. 'Anyway, she doesn't even know that I found out about the will's provisions.'

'So what were you going to do? Turn up on leap year's day with a surprise husband in tow and pretend you didn't know anything about the will? How were you going to explain his existence when you haven't even been dating anyone on a regular basis?'

Katherine's cheeks burned with humiliation that he should know so much about her non-existent social life. She could hardly tell him that it was his fault that she couldn't bring herself to accept dates with other men.

'That's why I thought of you,' she said quietly, silencing her conscience with the thought that at least she was telling a half-truth. 'They've heard about you at odd times over the last couple of years...when I've spoken about the hospital. And you met both my mother and my grandmother when we had the official opening of the new unit.'

It went without saying that such a good-looking doctor had made an impression on her relatives. She'd had to endure more than a couple of sly comments since they'd met him.

'So, exactly what are you proposing?' he enquired, and she knew she hadn't imagined the way he'd stressed the final word. 'That we tell them that after two years of working together we went to the Valentine's ball together and suddenly couldn't wait to get married?'

Disappointment tightened its hold on her throat and she had to wait a moment before she could reply.

'You don't have to be so sarcastic. If you don't want to do it you just have to say no. I won't even demand that you pay the forfeit.'

The attempt at humour fell flat.

'Forfeit? What, you mean, pay money into the hospital's coffers for turning you down?'

'Actually, according to some accounts, if you turn down a proposal of marriage you would have to give me a silk dress or a pair of kid gloves.'

'And cheap at the price,' he muttered, before falling silent again.

Katherine didn't know whether it was better to say something or to hold her tongue—the expression on Damon's face was giving nothing away.

Finally he released a long sigh and met her gaze again.

'What do the rules say about giving the proposee a little time to think about the proposal?'

She caught just a glimpse of turbulent emotions behind his air of quiet control. Suddenly she realised that he must be feeling just as pole-axed by the situation as she'd been when she'd first heard about her grandfather's will.

'Define "a little time",' she asked warily. 'There isn't very much time before it'll be too late to do anything.'

'Twenty-four hours?' he suggested.

The thought of having to wait that long before he gave her his answer was worse than waiting for the dentist to begin drilling, but it was only fair that he have time to think about it. After all, he hadn't refused her proposal...yet.

'Twenty-four hours,' she agreed. 'I'm working a late tomorrow—starting at one and finishing at nine.'

She half expected him to stand up as soon as she agreed; he wasn't a man who sat still for very long.

Obviously he was still deep in thought because several minutes passed while he sat, contemplating the swirling pattern in the lush carpet. From the frown drawing his dark brows together she guessed that he was troubled by those thoughts.

'I'm sorry, Damon,' she murmured, tentatively reaching out to touch the back of his clenched fist with the tips of her fingers. 'I know this isn't what you wanted for your life but…you were the only person I could think of to turn to.'

'Thanks for the compliment—I think,' he said wryly. 'Do you think it's time we went back in to rejoin the others?'

Katherine wasn't really in the mood for a large crowd of people pretending to act out the traditions of this special day, especially when she'd been forced into doing it for real.

'It's for a good cause,' he prompted, and she realised that his words could equally apply to both situations.

'Thank goodness it only happens once every four years,' she muttered as she levered herself up out of the settee, suddenly realising that it was far less comfortable than it looked.

Damon reached out to capture a fold of her skirt between his fingers and rubbed it gently.

'Silk, isn't it?' he commented and grinned, the unexpected mischief in his expression taking her by surprise. 'You wouldn't need me to buy you a silk dress if you've just bought one for yourself.'

'I could still do with a pair of really good gloves,' she said pointedly, hoping that he was only joking about the penalties of turning her down.

Katherine was surprised to see that the dancing was still in full swing when they returned to the ball. It seemed as though they'd been talking for hours out in the reception area.

'Where did you two disappear to?' Shari demanded as she swung past in the arms of a tall, red-headed man, but she didn't stay long enough to hear an answer.

The buffet was already being served at the far end of the room and Damon guided Katherine around the edge of the dance floor to avoid the crush of the more energetic dancers.

'What can I get you?' He gestured towards the mountains of food spread out enticingly over several long tables.

Mutely, she shook her head, her appetite non-existent.

'Something to drink? Soft drink? Alcohol?'

'Triple brandy?' she suggested, and was surprised into giggling by the shocked expression on his face. 'Well, I've heard it's good for giving people Dutch courage. Perhaps I should have taken it earlier this evening, then my stomach wouldn't be tied in knots now.'

'You're really that worried about your grandmother?'

The light was a little brighter at this end of the room so that people could see what they were choosing to eat, but she still couldn't see enough of his expression to guess at his thoughts.

'Actually, I think I'm on overload at the moment,' she admitted. 'I'm worried about the effect this will have on her health and her happiness. I'm upset that the two of them didn't feel they could tell me about it. I feel guilty for trying to drag you into the situation. I'm afraid that, just by asking you to…you know.' She glanced swiftly around in case anyone was taking notice of their conversation. 'I'm afraid that I've spoiled our friendship, that it'll never be the same again between us.'

'I must admit, it's the first time I've ever had a friend like you,' he said with a smile that gave her hopes a tiny lift. 'I can talk to you like a colleague *and* tease you like a little sister.'

To Katherine it was glaringly obvious that he'd

made no mention of any appreciation that she was a woman to whom he might be attracted, and her hopes sank back to the ground.

But was that what she wanted?

She'd known for two years that he wasn't attracted to her in the same way she was to him and had come to terms with it. This arrangement she'd just proposed wasn't for her own benefit but to save her grandmother from having to sell her beloved home.

The music in the background changed tempo suddenly.

'Hey! Rock and roll!' Damon exclaimed. 'Come on, little Kat, let's show this lot how it's done.'

Within seconds he'd dragged her out onto the dance floor and when she saw the wicked enjoyment in his grin she couldn't help responding.

She couldn't remember how long ago they'd discovered that they each had a secret passion for this type of dancing. What she did know was that each time they took to the floor together the time flew past fast and furiously and certainly didn't leave her a second free to think.

The first time Damon swung her high in the air there was a chorus of wolf-whistles that reminded her that her underwear was far from conventional for rock and roll.

She spared a fleeting word of thanks to her guardian angel that she'd decided against wearing the wickedly lacy set she'd been given for Christmas by her colleagues. She'd wondered if she might be in need of the artificial self-confidence they might lend her, but when the driving beat of the music lent wings to her feet she really didn't care.

This was the next best thing to making love with

Damon, their bodies moving together in perfect synchronisation, their blood pounding through their veins and their lungs straining for every breath.

One tune seemed to follow another without a break and the rest of the dancers had cleared a place in their midst, surrounding Damon and Katherine like spectators at an exhibition until finally the band wound up to their big finale.

Katherine was breathless and laughing and the applause started as Damon whooped and bent her back over his arm for a glorious Technicolor kiss.

Suddenly the room and everyone in it seemed to disappear. All she was conscious of was the warmth of his lips on hers in the first kiss they'd ever shared.

And it wasn't just his lips she was aware of. It was his arms holding her tightly against the curve of his body, her breasts pressed against the taut muscles of his chest, his thigh thrust between hers as he supported her weight, his hand cradling her head as the kiss exploded into fire.

It was still a few minutes before midnight but Katherine was already in her bed when there was a brief sharp rap at her door.

'Who on earth...?' She wasn't asleep but she was almost certain that it would be one of her colleagues eager to quiz her about the significance of that spectacular kiss. She'd almost decided to ignore the knock and pretend she was already asleep when it came again.

This time it was accompanied by a soft-voiced demand.

'Kat? Open up.'

There was only one person who called her Kat, and

with the realisation of who was standing outside her door Katherine's pulse went into overdrive.

What on earth was he doing here at this time of night? she thought as she felt for the switch to her bedside light.

'Come on, Kat,' he said impatiently with another knock, and she found herself scrabbling to force her arms into the tangled sleeves of her dressing-gown while she fought to escape the clutches of her bed-clothes.

'Damon. What do you want?' she breathed through a cautious gap between door and frame, horribly conscious that her hair must look like a rat's nest.

'Can I come in?' he asked softly, obviously aware that they were surrounded by potential eavesdroppers. 'It'll only take a minute.'

Suddenly she knew that he'd come to a decision and for one desperate second she was too frightened to let him tell her what it was because she was so certain that he was going to turn her down.

'Kat?' He was waiting patiently, and when she dared to meet his gaze it was almost as if he knew what she was thinking.

Slowly she pulled the door open and stepped aside, her bare feet almost silent on the floor.

Damon entered and swung the door closed behind him, and when she saw the way he dwarfed the space with his size and presence she realised that it was the first time he'd ever visited her room.

He was still wearing evening dress, his jacket and bow tie stark against the white of his shirt in the softly lit room.

'Um... Do you want to sit down?' she offered with a shaky gesture, then realised that with her clothing still draped over her chair the only place on offer was the tumbled mess of her bed.

'I won't stay,' he said, his voice sounding strangely husky in the silence of her room. 'We agreed on twenty-four hours but since I've made my decision I thought I ought to tell you before midnight—just in case you started demanding a forfeit.'

It felt as if she were breathing underwater as she tried to speak.

'And?'

The word was almost silent but he was watching her mouth as she formed it and she could almost feel the echoes of his kiss.

'And I accept your proposal,' he confirmed softly.

'You do?' she said on a gasp. 'Oh, Damon, I don't know how to thank you. You don't know how much this means to me.'

'Of course I do, Kat. That's why I agreed. Now, is it too late tonight to get down to the important things?'

'The important things?' she repeated faintly as she watched him shrugging his way out of his jacket, her mind suddenly filling with lurid pictures.

'Where will it be, the bed or the chair? On second thoughts, there isn't room on the chair.' He stepped around her and settled himself on the foot of her bed, his shoulders braced against the wall and his long legs stretched right out onto the small rug beside her bed.

'Come on, Kat,' Damon prompted while she stared in amazement at the sight of him making himself comfortable. It was almost as if he wasn't aware that she was wearing her nightclothes and that he was sprawled across the foot of her bed in his shirtsleeves.

He beckoned for her to come closer and she shivered with awareness but his words were prosaic. 'Tuck those chilly toes under the covers quickly, and help me make some decisions.'

'What decisions?' She felt as if she were wading through treacle as she approached the scene of all those X-rated dreams that she'd had about the wretched man. He'd said they were going to get down to the important things and her brain had immediately gone off on flights of wishful thinking. More fool her. It was only their arrangement he wanted to talk about.

'Well, the first and most important topic is how and when we tell your family,' he pointed out seriously. 'I know the deadline is two weeks away...'

'And one day,' she murmured numbly, suddenly wondering what sort of tornado she'd unleashed.

'And I take it that it's imperative that the two of them believe that you know nothing about the problem of the will?'

'God, yes!' *That* brought her out of her daze. 'If they thought I'd proposed marriage to you just so they could keep their home...' She shook her head.

'So it's up to the two of us to come up with a believable story to explain our sudden decision to marry. Then, no matter who asks awkward questions, we'll have to stick to it one hundred per cent.'

'Oh, but surely there's no reason why anyone at the hospital should know what we're doing. It could just be a secret between the two of us unless we go down to visit my family, couldn't it?'

He was shaking his head before she'd finished.

'It wouldn't work, Kat.'

'Why not? It's only going to be for a few weeks. Just until they do whatever has to be done with a will.'

Panic was flooding through her faster than a tidal

wave. How could she cope with pretending to be a blissful newly-wed in front of all their colleagues?

It would be bad enough having to pretend to her mother and grandmother that after two years of working together she and Damon were suddenly madly in love with each other, especially as she would also have to simultaneously pretend to Damon that it was all an act.

To have to keep it up for twenty-four hours a day under the eagle eyes of the rest of the hospital staff would be impossible.

'I don't know if you realise it, but sometimes it can take weeks, months or even years before a will finally goes through probate,' he warned, exasperatingly calm about the whole idea when she was just beginning to realise that she might have bitten off more than she could chew.

It wouldn't be so bad if she only felt the same degree of friendship for him that he felt for her.

The fact that she'd been more than half in love with him for the last two years had taken a serious turn with his devastating kiss earlier this evening. If she had to try to cope with pretending that they were completely starry-eyed over each other, all she could see on her horizon was heartbreak.

How could she ever face losing him once their arrangement came to an end?

Unfortunately, if Damon's logical deductions were right, there was going to be no alternative.

'Kat!'

She blinked. 'What?'

'I think you drifted off for a moment then. I know it's late but we've got to talk about this to get our stories straight before we tell anyone.'

Properly chastened, she made herself concentrate, all too aware that Damon was only going through this out of the goodness of his heart. She was the only one who was going to gain anything out of it…she and her family.

Within half an hour they'd come to an agreement about their basic story. The fact that they were both due for some time off later the next day meant that he would be able to drive the two of them down to break the news to her family in person.

Just the thought of trying to pull the wool over her grandmother's sharp eyes gave Katherine the shakes, but Damon seemed quite confident that they'd manage it.

'By the time we leave to visit them I should have finished making all the arrangements for the wedding, so we can present them with almost a *fait accompli*. As far as making an announcement at the hospital goes, the infamous grapevine will take care of that as soon as you tell your friends.'

Damon had to bring his hand up to cover an enormous yawn and Katherine wondered how he could possibly be feeling sleepy. She had so much adrenaline pouring through her she felt as if she'd be bouncing around the walls and off the ceiling for hours.

'Can you think of anything I've missed?' he asked as he lazily drew himself together and stood up, reaching across to retrieve his jacket.

She looked up at him, standing beside her bed with one finger through the loop of his jacket so that it draped casually over his shoulder, and was suddenly struck dumb by the idea that in two short weeks this gorgeous man was going to marry her. She couldn't possibly force her brain into thinking about making ar-

rangements for the event when she couldn't get over
the fact of it.

'Well, we're bound to think of something, even if
it's only hunting down birth certificates so we can apply for the licence. I'd better let you get back to bed
or neither of us will be fit for work tomorrow morning.'

Katherine scrambled out of bed and followed him
over to the door, intending to flip the catch on the lock
once he left the room.

'Oh, I nearly forgot,' he said, stopping and turning
towards her so suddenly that she nearly ploughed into
him. 'We're going to have to put in a bit of practice
at this or we're not going to be fooling anyone.'

Before she could ask what he was talking about he'd
cradled her cheek in one warm palm and was brushing
a gentle kiss across her startled lips.

'Mmm. Nice,' he murmured, his words a direct echo
of his response to her new dress this evening.

She wanted to contradict him; wanted to tell him that
even such a brief contact between their mouths was
more than merely nice when he parted his lips and
angled his head to deepen the contact.

It was a hot, bold kiss that quickly had her clinging
to him and, as if she'd been struck by lightning twice
in one night, she didn't know whether her brain would
ever recover.

Even when he drew away and murmured a husky
goodnight she was struggling to force her eyelids open
and only managed it when she heard the decisive click
of her door closing.

'Hey! Kat, wait a minute!'

She'd had her hand on the door of Windermere

Ward, ready to push it open, when she heard Damon's voice calling her from along the corridor behind her.

Instantly, her heartbeat doubled and she began to tremble but she forced herself to turn and face him.

Why did the wretched man have to look so gorgeous? He couldn't have had any more sleep than she had but he was striding along as if he had energy to spare.

'We forgot something last night,' he began when he drew closer, beckoning her away from the ward entrance. 'I don't know if you want to wait until we go to see your family this evening or whether you'd rather get used to it today?'

Katherine hadn't a clue what he was talking about. All she could think about was that stunning kiss—until he reached into his pocket and took out a small, well-worn velvet box.

Her breath caught in her throat when he flipped the lid open to reveal a dainty ring, two diamonds flanking a sapphire almost the exact shade of his eyes.

'I don't know if it's to your taste, but it belonged to my mother and I thought…'

'Oh, Damon, it's beautiful,' she whispered as her eyes filled with emotional tears. 'I couldn't have chosen anything more perfect. I promise I'll look after it carefully.'

One half of her was thrilled that she would be wearing something so beautiful and of such sentimental value to Damon; the other half wanted to weep buckets that the whole thing was just make-believe.

'Does that mean I get another kiss?' he teased with a wicked grin just as the ward doors were thumped open by an aggressive young shoulder.

'Bloody doctors,' swore a young voice that wavered

uncertainly between tenor and soprano. 'And bloody nurses, too.'

'Good morning, Frank,' Damon said without missing a beat, almost as if kissing her had been the furthest thing from his mind.

Katherine was only grateful that their trouble-making patient hadn't come out just a few seconds later. It would have been bad enough if he'd caught the suggestive wink Damon had just thrown at her, but if he'd caught the pair of them kissing they'd never have heard the end of it.

'What's so good about it?' Frank demanded with an aggressive flourish of one of his crutches. 'There were a whole lot of drunk drivers about last night and the operating theatre is full so *my* surgery had to be put off—for the second time. I'm *never* going to get out of this place…not until I'm getting my old-age pension.'

'Oh, I think we'll manage to get it done before then,' Katherine said with a chuckle. 'You don't think that I actually *want* to keep you on my ward, the way you keep getting everybody into trouble?'

'Well, I've got to do *something* to liven this place up. It's just so *boring,* with everyone just lying about all day.'

'It'll be your turn to lie about when you've had your operation done,' Damon pointed out. 'It's a fairly major job and you certainly won't be slamming your way through ward doors for a while, crutches or no crutches.'

'Yeah, but at least it'll be getting better then, won't it? At the moment I'm having to gimp about on these things, knowing it's all to come, while the rest of the team are winning games without me. I was their best goal-scorer till this happened.'

Katherine felt sorry for the youngster. He'd broken his leg in a collision on a football field and the bones hadn't united properly, leaving him with a shorter, deformed lower leg with his foot stuck out at an unnatural angle.

The orthopaedic consultant had decided that the only way of correcting the situation was to re-break the bones and reposition them, using an adjustable external fixator to allow for the bones to be 'stretched' back to their proper length.

Now the problem was the amount of time the operation was going to take and the lack of time available in Theatre with an apparently full list of emergency cases.

'Do you want me to see if I can find out how long you're likely to have to wait?' Damon offered as he surreptitiously began to usher Frank back towards the ward.

'They might tell you more than they tell the nurses, you being a doctor and all,' Frank said, apparently oblivious of the fact that Katherine might take umbrage at his slighting tone.

'In the meantime, have you had your breakfast yet?' she asked. 'I've noticed that young men are always more likely to snarl and growl when they haven't been fed recently.'

'I didn't want to eat anything in case they got a space in the operating theatre and it stopped me from having the operation.'

'Good thinking,' Damon said with a grin. 'But if there's going to be more than a twelve-hour delay you might as well make the most of the food before it all disappears. We can always review the situation again before you're due to eat your lunch.'

'OK, Doc,' the youngster conceded with a grudging grin, just a faint shadow of his usual broad beam. 'I'll go and sit down like a good little boy until you come and tell me what's going on. Then we can take it from there.'

'Good enough,' Damon said with a grin of his own. 'I'll get right on it.'

'Oh, by the way, Frank,' Katherine added. 'Just one more thing for you to think about. Some of the people waiting to go to Theatre were the innocent victims of those drunks. It's not their fault they've taken your place, any more than it's Windy's staff's fault.'

She'd kept her tone gentle, knowing that he'd been disappointed before, but for all his mischief he was an intelligent lad. By the time she'd finished speaking his attitude had undergone a visible change.

'I know, Sister,' he admitted, rather shamefaced. 'I'm sorry.'

'Enough said.' She nodded in the direction of the table at which all the mobile patients shared their mealtimes. 'Go and make yourself scarce for a moment. OK?'

'And all without raising your voice,' Damon murmured softly with a chuckle in his voice. 'Scary lady.'

He gestured for her to precede him as they made their way towards the office and she discovered that, although she'd left her room in plenty of time, after the dual delay in the corridor she was only just in time for handover.

Charge Nurse Lenny Price had been on duty overnight, and while he started giving Katherine a rundown of the status on each of the ward's occupants and any changes in their drugs she found herself over-whelmingly aware of the fact that Damon had followed her and was now standing right behind her.

He waited until Lenny had finished before he asked for an update on the likelihood of Frank making it up to Theatre in the near future.

'All I got was a message not to give him his pre-meds instead of his breakfast because all the electives had gone out of the window with the influx of emergencies,' Lenny said.

'Well, he's in a real strop about it and wants to know how long he's likely to be held back before he'll consent to eat his breakfast.'

'I was following him when he slammed his way out of the department, but when I saw the two of you out there I left you to it,' Lenny admitted. 'Do you think it will do any good if you give a ring upstairs to find out how many hours they reckon it's going to be?'

'It's worth a try,' Damon said as he reached for the phone.

'It might make him a little easier to live with if he thinks we're chasing it for him,' Katherine said hopefully. 'Otherwise, heaven only knows what sort of mischief he'll get up to on the ward while he's waiting to hear about his operation.'

'It wouldn't be so bad if he didn't involve the rest of the ward. He even incites the sane and sensible ones to riot over the silliest things,' Lenny pointed out glumly, then brightened visibly. 'Still, it's not going to be my problem for another thirteen hours, so I wish you well of him. Have a lovely day, both of you.'

Katherine was about to follow him out of the room to leave Damon to his phone call, keen to begin her usual visit to each of her young charges, when Damon grabbed her elbow and signalled for her to wait. She could tell from the grimace he pulled that the message from his phone call wasn't very hopeful, but his first words when he put the phone down were nothing to do with Frank's operation.

'You didn't answer my question,' he said softly, pulling her inexorably closer by the hand wrapped warmly round her arm.

Distracted by the physical contact between them, the only question she could remember him asking her was whether he could have a kiss. With nerves sticking her tongue firmly to the roof of her mouth there was no way she could answer.

'Did you want to put this on now or would you rather wait until this evening when we go to tell your family?' he said patiently as he held the small box out on the palm of his hand.

'Th-this evening, please,' she stammered, almost disappointed that he hadn't been talking about that kiss.

Then he dipped his head and stole one anyway.

Fleeting as it was, it wasn't swift enough to avoid Shari's eagle eyes as she entered the room.

'What's this? What's this?' she demanded with obvious delight. 'Have the two of you got some sort of Valentine's Day hangover? I've heard the symptoms can be very dangerous for your emotional health. Now, then, tell Auntie Shari what's going on.'

CHAPTER THREE

'WHAT a day!' Katherine groaned as she settled back into the comfort of the passenger seat.

They were setting off on time to make the hour's journey to visit her family, but only by dint of sneaking out before they could be trapped by a 'surprise' party.

Katherine had caught wind of it amid all the gossip resulting from Shari's inopportune arrival.

'It was all your fault, you know,' Katherine grumbled as she relived every one of the dozens of congratulatory hugs she'd received. 'If you'd kept your distance Shari would never have guessed what was going on.'

'It was bound to come out sooner or later,' Damon pointed out calmly. 'In fact, it's probably worked out for the best if we can drop hints that everyone at the hospital already knows. It makes it seem as if it's something we've been contemplating for some time, rather than a last-minute plan to foil your grandfather's will.'

The reminder that this whole scenario was just part of an enormous hoax was sobering. In the excitement whirling around the two of them all morning it had been all too easy to let herself imagine that they'd embarked on a real engagement because they were in love with each other.

Damon had certainly played his part to perfection.

'Unless you've changed your mind?' he questioned

suddenly, his voice gritty as he concentrated on the road ahead.

Was that a subtle hint? Had he changed his mind about helping her now that he realised exactly how public everything was becoming? He'd certainly been right when he'd told her there was no way they could keep something like this from their colleagues. The whole thing had turned into a three-ring circus.

'Have you?' she retorted, fear turning her voice thready in the confines of the car. Did he want to back out on her? If he did, how would she be able to save her grandmother's home? After today's commotion she had no options left. She'd never be able to convince anyone that within the space of two weeks she'd jilted Damon in favour of another man.

'I gave my word that I'd help you,' he confirmed softly. 'Until you convince me that you no longer need my help, my promise will stand.'

'Thank you,' she said formally, while a mountain of doubts and fears rolled off her back.

She knew that there were going to be myriad problems ahead of them, but if they were both committed to the path ahead, perhaps they could solve them together. All she could do was cross her fingers and hope.

'I can see why your grandmother doesn't want to leave it,' Damon commented as he drew up in front of the house.

Katherine took a critical look at the house she'd known all her life and saw how impressive it would look to a stranger.

Although not that old, it was vaguely Tudor in design and looked as if it had stood there for ever, offering comfort and shelter.

'Grandfather always insisted on keeping the fabric of the house in good repair but the décor inside is all my grandmother's doing. It's just such a *comfortable* house to live in.'

'Well, I can see curtains twitching at that window over there so they must have heard us arrive. Are you ready to give the performance of your life?'

Damon's reminder that this was all just an act for him was enough to stiffen her resolve and she released her seat belt and reached for the door.

'Darling! What a lovely surprise!' exclaimed the petite woman who opened the door and beckoned them in.

It had always been obvious from the identical shapes of their faces and the honey brown colour of their eyes that Katherine took after her mother in her looks. It was equally obvious that she'd inherited her slender height from the grandmother who waited for them in the warmth of the sitting room.

'Welcome to Hillsboro' House,' the older woman said with an outstretched hand. 'It's Dr Cade, isn't it?'

'Please, call me Damon,' he invited as he waited for the ladies to take their seats. 'What a lovely room this is—so welcoming, and with that wonderful view towards the hills.'

Ever the gracious hostess, her grandmother took charge of the conversation, telling Damon of her efforts over the years to preserve and enhance just that view.

Katherine found she couldn't contribute a single word. All she could think about was the moment when one of her relatives finally asked why the two of them had come visiting so unexpectedly.

With a sudden jolt she realised that Damon had forgotten to give her his mother's ring. They hadn't even tried it on to see if it fitted her finger. What would her grandmother think when they hadn't even managed to get the basic props in position for the performance?

Suddenly she felt Damon's hand capture hers where it lay on her lap and she jumped as though she'd touched a live electric cable.

'Actually,' he was saying, and just the tone of his voice made her stomach clench with apprehension, 'I know it's a little early in the afternoon but we've brought a bottle of champagne with us. We'd like the two of you to join us in celebrating our engagement.'

As he'd been speaking he'd drawn the little box out of his pocket and flipped it open to lift the ring out.

Katherine watched in breathless silence as he slid it onto her third finger, feeling a strange kind of resignation when she realised that it was a perfect fit.

'Oh, my goodness…!'

'Oh, Katherine…!'

She was distantly aware that there was a confused jumble of exclamations going on somewhere in the room but her attention was totally captured by the intent expression on Damon's face.

His sapphire blue eyes had darkened as he gazed down at her and with a sweet sense of anticipation she just knew that he was going to kiss her again.

Even the knowledge that her mother and grandmother were watching didn't stop her melting against him, her hands creeping up to link behind his neck.

When the tip of Damon's tongue teased her own and tempted it to join his in a mutual exploration she knew that he was as lost in the sensations building between them as she was.

It was only the sound of an insistent cough that

broke through their concentration on each other, effectively dousing the steadily building conflagration.

Even when they drew back from each other Damon's eyes were fixed intently on her and she knew he must be able to see the blush as it spread from her throat up into her cheeks.

'Well, my dears,' her grandmother said with a very pleased smile, 'this is such a surprise. Katherine, why haven't you brought Damon down to visit us before if this was the way things were going? He could have stayed with us last weekend, instead of coming down for such a flying visit.'

'That's my fault,' Damon said, filling the silence swiftly when Katherine couldn't find either her voice or any explanation that wouldn't reveal the secret. 'I think Katherine finally got tired of waiting for me to propose, so last night she took advantage of the date and turned the tables on me. What could I do but accept?' he finished, his voice husky as he lifted her hand and planted a swift kiss on the finger bearing his ring.

'Actually, it was my grandmother's fault,' Katherine said, hastily breaking into speech in an attempt at ignoring the treacherous emotions that threatened to overwhelm her. 'Do you remember, last weekend when I was home? You were talking about all the customs and superstitions that have been dying out over the years since you were a girl. You were the one who told me about the woman's right to propose in a leap year and the penalties for a refusal.'

It wasn't until she'd finished speaking that she realised how tense Damon had been. Had he been worried that she was about to let slip the conversation she'd overheard?

Almost immediately he stood up and went to retrieve

the bottle of champagne from the car—when had he had time to buy it, for heaven's sake? Katherine breathed a silent sigh of relief when her mother went to fetch the best set of glasses.

At least the sudden exodus would give her a chance to collect her scattered thoughts. She was also grateful that it meant she only had to face her grandmother while she did it, but when she saw the intent expression on that formidable lady's face she began to wish for Damon's speedy return.

'Well, Katherine. What a dark horse you are,' she murmured softly, and beckoned her to come closer.

Once more she was enveloped in the familiar scent of English lavender as her grandmother gave her a hug.

'Sit here, child,' she said as she patted the arm of the chair. 'Tell me all about it. You love him to bits, of course.'

'Of course,' Katherine echoed with a bitter-sweet smile, knowing that it was nothing more than the truth.

Suddenly, she realised that in spite of the bogus nature of her arrangement with Damon there was going to be a hidden bonus for her. For however long their relationship lasted, she could openly and honestly proclaim her feelings for him without fearing that it would frighten him away. Only *he* would believe that she was merely playing a part.

'I thought there was something going on between the two of you,' she said with a satisfied nod. 'His was the name you always mentioned most often when you were talking about your work at the hospital. It was always Damon this and Damon that but it never seemed to get any further. I was beginning to wonder if it was all one-sided. Now...'

She reached for Katherine's hand, obviously wanting to have a closer look at the ring.

'Oh, my. It's so pretty and dainty. He's obviously got very good taste because it suits you perfectly.'

'Thank you for the compliment, but I can't really accept it,' Damon admitted as he entered the room, carrying a silver tray bearing four champagne flutes and the opened bottle. 'My father gave the ring to my mother when he asked her to marry him and she wore it proudly till the day she died. Since then it's been sitting in its little box, just waiting for the right person to come along to bring it to life again.'

If Katherine hadn't known better she would have thought he was telling the truth. As it was, she was realising that he was a far better actor than she'd ever expected.

Unfortunately, that made her wonder whether he'd been acting when he'd been kissing her, too. Had he really been as affected by the experience as he'd appeared, or had it all been pretence?

'Well, my dears, here's to a long and happy life together,' Katherine's grandmother proposed as she lifted her glass towards them. 'May you always be as happy as you are today.'

'To Katherine and Damon,' her mother said with a misty smile. 'Have the two of you had any thoughts about setting the date yet?'

Katherine nearly choked on her champagne. This was the moment when the whole scheme could fall apart. If the two of them suspected that she'd overheard them talking, this would be when they put two and two together and made a disastrous four.

'Actually,' Damon said thoughtfully, as if he were just now contemplating the issue, 'the two of us have known each other for a couple of years already so there doesn't seem to be much point in a long delay. What do you think?' he prompted Katherine.

'What are you suggesting?' she asked, following his lead and hoping she was feeding him the right lines. It seemed as if he didn't want her to appear too eager.

'Well, you finally proposed to me on Valentine's Day in a leap year, so it seems only fitting that we should get married on leap year's day.'

'But that's only a couple of weeks away. We could never get anything organised that quickly, could we?'

'You could if we helped,' her mother interrupted quickly.

'But what about all the things that take so long to make? The cake? The dress? And how about making a booking for the ceremony?'

'My dear, in the sandalwood chest in my room is the dress I wore when I married your grandfather. You're about the same height and size I was then so, if you wanted, we could see if we could make the necessary alterations...'

Katherine was speechless, her eyes filling with tears so that the whole room began to blur.

'I think that means yes,' Damon said, wrapping an arm round her and pulling her close to his side. 'Now all we need to know is if she agrees to the date.'

'If I didn't know better, I'd think I dreamed that conversation between my mother and grandmother,' Katherine said.

Finally, they were on their way back to the hospital again and she'd had time to think over the strange afternoon and evening.

'What do you mean?' Damon was little more than a

silhouette beside her in the car, his face briefly lit by flashes of light as cars went past in the opposite direction.

She glanced across at him, wondering at the edgy tone to his voice, then looked away again. She didn't need bright light to know what he looked like.

From the first time she'd met him she'd been struck by the lean intelligence of his face and the dark intensity in his deep blue eyes. The fact that just one glance from those eyes was more potent than a deliberate seduction attempt from any other man was just her misfortune.

'Well, the conversation I overheard was fairly fraught. The two of them were both worried out of their minds about having to sell their home. Now, just a few days later, there's been no mention of it. Surely, now that they know we're getting married, they would have said *something*?'

'Perhaps one event has driven the other out of their minds, or perhaps they've reasoned that, as you're getting married, they don't need to worry about it any more.'

'And the only way I could find out would be to ask them point blank.'

'And that would let them know that you'd overheard them and ruin all your plans,' he finished for her. 'You're just going to have to compose your soul in patience and wait till all the legalities have been sorted out. You'll probably be able to find that out later from your grandfather's solicitor.'

Katherine subsided into a troubled silence. Damon was probably right, but she had a very uncomfortable feeling about the whole situation.

Obviously, her mother wasn't going to advise caution when time was of the essence, but she and Katherine's grandmother had certainly thrown themselves into the discussions about the upcoming marriage with a vengeance.

It had been quite embarrassing how eager they'd been to drag her up to her grandmother's room to try on the carefully preserved wedding dress.

She remembered her first glimpse of the precious garment. The photographs of that long-ago wedding hadn't done it justice. With the passing years, the heavy peau-de-soie silk had turned a delicate shade of ivory but the intricate embroidery emphasising the Empire line and long fitted sleeves had stayed almost as pale and perfect as the day the last stitch had been finished.

The starkly simple style was going to need very little alteration to ensure a good fit. Even the long gossamer-fine veil still appeared to be intact.

'Is the dress silk?' Damon asked suddenly, startling her with the evidence that their thoughts must have been following similar tracks.

'Yes. It's yellowed slightly with age but it looks wonderful...and it's going to fit. Why did you ask?'

'Well, I was wondering about the logistics of it,' he said, far too casually to be believed. 'If I'd turned your proposal down I would have had to buy you a silk dress, so it seems only right that as I accepted you have to provide a silk dress to get married in.'

It only took Katherine half a second to realise that he was teasing, and with their shared laughter the strange air of tension seemed to disappear.

By the time he pulled up outside the accommodation block where she lived they were actually holding a completely ordinary conversation.

'We're going to have to do something about your

room,' he said as he released his seat belt, and in an instant the tension was back.

'Why? What's wrong with it?' she demanded.

'Well, for a start, your bed's not nearly big enough for the two of us,' he pointed out with a sexy grin. 'It would be far better if you moved into my flat...unless you'd rather look for somewhere new?'

'Why would I want to move? My room's convenient for getting to work and—' Suddenly she realised what he was talking about and she was surprised that the whole interior of the car didn't light up with the fiery blush that heated her cheeks. 'You mean, after the wedding,' she finished lamely.

'I've got a spare room in my flat but it's very tiny and there's no bed in it because I've been using it as a study-cum-office. Anyway, my bed is a very large double.'

Katherine could imagine that someone of his height *would* need more than her single bed to sleep in and she had no difficulty at all imagining him sprawled out across that very large double bed of his, even though she'd never seen it.

'Can we decide about that another day?' she begged, chickening out of discussing, even remotely, the limited intimacies that even *their* unusual marriage would involve. 'I think I reached overload point somewhere round the heated discussion about my bouquet.'

In the dark she heard Damon groan his sympathy then they both chuckled at the memory of the two ladies going politely head to head over their rival preferences.

'Thank you for saying that you wanted to provide my flowers. I think we'd still be there as referees, otherwise.'

'You're welcome. But about your room... I think you'll find that you need to hand in your notice to the hospital or you might have to keep paying rent even after you've moved out. Still, I expect tomorrow will be soon enough.'

Suddenly she felt him thread his fingers between hers and lift her captured hand to his lips.

She shouldn't be surprised because he'd always seemed to find it easy to touch people, but this new habit of kissing her was going to take a while to get used to. It wasn't as if there was anyone nearby who needed convincing...but perhaps he felt he needed to practise the sort of affectionate gestures others would expect to see.

'I-I really ought to get some sleep,' she stammered, overwhelmed by all the things she was trying not to think about. It was going to be bad enough keeping the essentials in order in the mess that used to be her well-organised brain.

'Hey, Sister, have you heard?' Frank called across to her as she arrived on the ward the next day.

'No, Frank. Heard what?' Katherine allowed her feet to take her on a detour towards their most ebullient patient, surprised to see him in his bed. There was time to find out what was going on as there were still another ten minutes before she was officially on duty.

'I'm going down to Theatre today,' he crowed, almost bouncing around the room in his elation. 'They finished all the emergency ones and I'm going to be done today. See, I've already got this stupid dress-thing on.' He plucked at the blue-striped fabric. 'My mum and dad have been here for a couple of hours already.

They've just gone for a cup of coffee but they're going to come up to Theatre with me until I go to sleep.'

'You mean I'm actually going to have a bit of peace and quiet for a change?' she taunted, silently delighted that he was finally going to have his long-awaited operation. 'I can't wait till you've had your pre-med.'

'Had it,' he said with a cheeky grin and she groaned.

'Trust you to be one of the ones who doesn't go all dozy and quiet!' she exclaimed. 'How much longer before the porters come to take you away?'

'Dunno.' He shrugged. 'Shall I go and find out?'

'No, thank you.' She had to grab him by the arm to stop him sliding out of bed. 'You stay where you are, or the porters might think you've changed your mind and go on to the next one on the list. *I*'ll find out what's happening.'

'Thanks, Sister. I'll be good,' he promised.

'That'll be the day,' Katherine murmured under her breath as she redirected her path towards the office. It would only take a phone call to find out what she needed to know.

Shari was behind the desk but before she could say a word two arms encircled her from behind and pulled her back against a very warm, very solid male body.

'Hello, beautiful. Sleep well?' demanded a familiar voice in her ear.

'Damon! You made me jump,' she complained, horribly aware that not only was she blushing in front of one of her best friends, but she was also wishing that friend could disappear into thin air so she could enjoy the sensation of having Damon's arms wrapped around her.

'Should I kiss you better?' he offered, but she wasn't having any of that. Not when she was on the ward.

'I'm here to find out when Frank is due in Theatre,' she said briskly, at the same time taking hold of each of Damon's arms and removing them from around her waist. 'Any chance you could do a quick phone call and find out—before he decides it'll be quicker to walk up there than wait for the porters?'

'I'll do it straight away,' Shari promised. 'You've still got a couple of minutes before hand-over, so you can say hello to your fiancé. I promise I won't peep.'

Katherine groaned at the theatrical gesture when Shari ostentatiously swivelled the chair away from the desk so that she wasn't facing them any more.

Damon didn't seem to realise that her friend was only teasing when he immediately pulled her into his arms again.

'Damon!' she muttered half-heartedly. 'She's not watching so you don't have to—'

'Put your claws away, Kat. She's watching our reflection in the window,' he murmured, just before he curved one hand around her cheek and tilted her head.

Katherine gazed up into his face and knew without a doubt that he was going to kiss her. She also knew that as soon as his lips touched hers she would completely forget that it was all just an act.

'Hey, you two, the room's filling with steam!' Shari called a century or two later, her voice filled with laughter. 'How you ever kept a lid on this for the last two years I'll never know.'

'Um, I'll just go and tell Frank about his operation,' Katherine muttered, seriously doubting that her legs were going to work properly.

'It might be an idea if you asked me what the answer was from Theatre first,' Shari pointed out with a giggle.

'Honestly, you're worse than some of the kids we get in here, but they've got an excuse…they're teenagers!'

Katherine flung her hands up in the air in disgust. 'All right, then, deliver your own message. I'll be waiting here when you come back for hand-over. And as for you…' She turned on Damon, her hands on her hips. 'Haven't you got something urgent to do somewhere else?'

'Yes. But you're due on duty here and it'd be no fun without you,' he retorted, then had to duck out of the way quickly when she threatened to hit him.

Shari, damn her, could hardly stop laughing.

Katherine was able to regain her equilibrium during the first half of her shift, especially as Damon seemed to have completely disappeared.

It helped that she was kept busy.

Until Frank was finally wheeled out of the ward he kept up a constant stream of comments, in spite of his parents' best efforts to keep him quiet. Katherine made certain to let them know that no one really minded.

'We realised long ago that it's just the way Frank was made,' she reassured his mother. 'There's absolutely no malice in him and he really keeps the rest of the patients alert, even if it's only to persuade them to drive the staff round the bend!'

The next patient in line was Laurel Kent and she was far more nervous about her upcoming turn in Theatre.

Katherine was watching as the youngster grew quieter and quieter and knew that it had little to do with her pre-med.

Finally she went across and drew the curtains around the bed for a semblance of privacy. She'd brought an extra chair with her and sat down on the other side of the bed from Laurel's mother.

'I hope you don't mind, Mrs Kent, but I've been watching Laurel and I need to ask her a question.' She reached for the pretty youngster's hand and gave it a reassuring squeeze. 'Laurel, are you sure you want to have this operation? It's not too late to change your mind if you want to.'

Laurel gaped at her and Mrs Kent started to speak but Katherine held up her hand.

'I know it's taken a long time to get this far, Mrs Kent, and I know the operation will make a lot of difference to Laurel's life, but if she's not ready for it yet then we need to know.'

She turned back to her patient. 'I know you're only sixteen, but you're almost an adult now. I know some adults would like to believe you're all little kids until you get to twenty-one, but I believe you're old enough to have a say in the decisions that affect your life. Do you agree?'

The reply was slow in coming but Katherine knew by the change in the youngster's expression that she quite liked the concept.

'Yes. I agree,' she said softly. 'I'm old enough to know what I want.'

'But—' Mrs Kent started, her hands knotting together in agitation.

'Please, Mum.' This time it was Laurel who asked her mother to wait. 'How do you see my choices, Sister? What decisions can I make?'

'Well, your basic choice is whether you have the operation done today or not. You already know it's going to mean months of discomfort but to make your choice you have to decide whether the *you* that will exist after the operation is the person you want to be, or whether you would prefer to stay as you are now.'

There was complete silence within the arbour of the drawn curtains as Laurel looked down at herself in the bed first then across at her mother.

Katherine's eyes followed the same course, noting the abnormally short bones in the youngster's legs, which had resulted from her achondroplasia, and then comparing them with her mother's more average stature.

The silence seemed to stretch out endlessly and Katherine began to wonder if she'd made a mistake when she'd approached Laurel's obvious fears in this way. Then the youngster reached for her mother's hand.

'Yes. I'm ready to have it done today,' she said firmly. 'I know it won't make me as tall as you are, Sister, but even a few inches taller than I am now will help me to fit in better with the rest of the world.'

She gave Katherine a shaky grin. 'I bet you're about five feet six inches,' she challenged. 'You've probably never known what it's like to have to grab someone in a supermarket to reach for something on the top shelf.'

'You're right there,' Katherine admitted. 'I was always the tall, skinny one at school, but that had its own drawbacks. It meant I never had the excuse for walking up to some gorgeous-looking man and begging him to help me.' She batted her eyelashes coyly to make Laurel giggle.

'I'll have to practise that,' the young girl said with a much more genuine smile. 'After all, five feet two is still small enough to *pretend* I need help, isn't it?'

Katherine took her leave, pulling the curtains back

before she went. After that little episode she was looking forward to a cup of coffee.

'Until this week I never realised how much you like
walking on tightropes,' Damon said over his shoulder
as she entered the staffroom in search of a clean mug.
'I was holding my breath on the other side of those
curtains, waiting for Laurel to speak.'

He turned round with a steaming mug in each hand.
'I was going to bring this through to your office but
you may as well put your feet up while you've got the
chance. It'll give us a few minutes to talk.'

CHAPTER FOUR

KATHERINE lowered herself warily onto one end of the two-seater settee.

Her hand tightened around the handle of her drink at the same time as her stomach tightened itself into knots. There had been something about the way Damon had said it was time they talked that had had that effect on her, and that was a shame. For two years they'd had a wonderfully relaxed relationship and that had all been spoiled now.

'How is Frank doing?' she asked in a last-ditch attempt at setting the conversation off in a different direction.

'As well as can be expected,' he parroted with an old-fashioned look that said she knew almost as much as he did about the youngster's operation.

She flushed when she realised that he'd seen straight through her, and was summoning up an apology when he began again.

'Katherine...look, *we* know that this whole wedding thing is a ploy to help your family keep their home, but that doesn't mean we can afford to play at it. If we're going to persuade the lawyers that we're not committing some sort of fraud, we've got to behave as if the whole thing is real.'

'Fraud?' she repeated weakly. 'Surely it's not fraud if it means my grandmother gets to stay in the house she's lived in most of her life.'

'Until the will has gone through probate, I think the

house still officially belongs to your grandfather and is therefore his to dispose of as he wishes. Just because you don't like his decision…'

'It's so unfair,' she burst out, interrupting him. 'He *knew* how much my grandmother loved it. Why would he force her to leave it at her age?'

'Perhaps his brain was starting to go and he didn't realise what he was doing,' Damon suggested. 'If so, your grandmother could have grounds for contesting the will.'

Katherine shook her head, knowing it was impossible.

'She'd never do it. It would mean telling the world that he'd become a crazy old man, and she'd rather lose her home than do that.'

'Loyalty,' he said with an understanding smile. 'She's obviously passed the concept on to you or you'd never have come up with this scheme.'

Katherine could have groaned when she realised that the conversation had circled neatly back to where it had started.

'OK, Damon,' she said in resignation, turning sideways to look at him across the narrow width of the settee. 'What was it we needed to talk about?'

'I had a phone call from your mother.'

'What?' she gasped. 'When? Was she ringing up to tell you that they know what's going on?'

'Not a bit of it. It seemed far more like a "welcome to the family" sort of conversation.'

'What else did she say? I can tell from your face that it was more than that.'

'She said that she and your grandmother were sorry we weren't going to have a big summer wedding in the local church. They quite understood why we would choose the hospital chapel and were looking forward to attending, but in return they insisted that they were going to give us a honeymoon.'

'A honeymoon?' Katherine felt her eyes grow enormous as she stared at him in horror. 'What have they done?'

'Nothing too horrendous, as far as they can see. In fact, it might work out to be a godsend. There won't be anyone else around so we can just be ourselves.'

'Don't go all cryptic on me,' she snapped. '*What* have they done?'

'Claws away, Kat,' he said with a grin, and she felt like using them on him for real. She was still contemplating the idea when he continued, 'They've given us free run of their home while they indulge in a weekend of shopping and visiting friends. Your mother assured me that everything would be left ready, with the fridge and freezer full and plenty of wine to choose from.'

'Thank God that's all it is,' she sighed and allowed herself to relax. 'For one awful moment I thought you were going to say that they were going to be there in the house, watching us. There's no way that we could have explained sleeping in separate beds.'

Damon grimaced wryly. 'Apart from that, I can report that I've spoken to the hospital chaplain, my best suit has been sent to the dry-cleaner, the flowers have been ordered and I've arranged an appointment to see the registrar because we're going to need a special licence.'

'And all I've managed to do is hand in my notice for my room,' she admitted.

'Any problem?'

'Apparently, I should have given a month's notice, but in the circumstances, and in view of the fact that she's got someone waiting to snap it up, I've got away with it.'

'So you can start moving your stuff as soon as you like,' he suggested. 'It doesn't really make sense to leave it all till the last minute.'

Suddenly Katherine had the unnerving feeling that she was standing directly in the path of a speeding train. It wasn't Damon's fault, of course. *She* was the one who had set the wretched thing in motion and had been so certain that she was in control.

Why was she now getting the feeling that someone should have warned her that the brakes weren't working?

She returned to the ward just in time for Frank to arrive from his spell in post-op.

'Welcome back, Frank,' Katherine said as she checked his post-operative notes. 'Have they given you enough painkillers?'

'I'm all right,' he said, his speech slightly slurred and definitely less ebullient than before.

'Hey, don't go getting all macho on me,' she insisted. 'You could slow your recovery down if you're in too much pain.'

He grunted. 'It's beginning to ache a bit,' he admitted. 'A bit like toothache when it starts to come back to life after the dentist.'

'You probably don't remember at the moment, but I explained about the special pain relief we were going to give you after your operation.' Katherine brought his hand across to the special pump filled with a syringe of analgesic drugs.

The fine capillary would feed a measured dose straight into his vein each time the button was pressed.

'Here's the button for you to press,' she explained

as she positioned his finger. 'You can't give yourself too much because the little pump won't allow you to use it again before it's safe to do so. This way, I won't have to keep giving you injections and you won't have to have any more drugs than you need.'

'I remember,' he said, his eyes already brighter as he focused on the gadget. 'You mean I'm really in control of this myself? I can use as much or as little as I like.'

'Within the safety limits, yes. And we only give them to the patients who are adult enough to cope with them so you can take it as a compliment.'

Frank tried to shift in the bed to get a better look at the pump and gasped.

'Ow!' He grimaced. 'Well, that was a very grown-up pain.'

He deliberately pressed the button and Katherine heard the pump mechanism deliver the required dose of medication.

'How long did you say it takes before that stuff works?' he muttered, his eyes drooping again.

'Soon,' she promised. 'It'll probably make you sleep, too, so when you wake up again your parents will probably be sitting right beside you.'

'Mum kissed me before I went into Theatre,' he said with a scowl. 'I hope no one saw her getting sloppy. It would ruin my street cred, especially with the others on the team.'

'Don't worry. The Theatre staff won't have noticed. They get special training in turning the other way when mums get sloppy.'

'Duh!' he muttered scathingly with an attempt at a grin, but he was already more asleep than awake.

Katherine quickly did his next set of observations

herself just to put her own mind at rest, then handed
Frank's care over to one of the more junior nurses.

A minor riot broke out when two youngsters started
arguing about who had cheated in their computer game
and Katherine had to hurry across to act as mediator.

Neither Liam nor Sam would admit to being in the
wrong and it looked as if the situation was going to
escalate just in time for the visitors to arrive.

Katherine was growing impatient with the two of
them. She had far more important things to do than
play piggy-in-the-middle.

'All right, then, I've found a solution,' she said suddenly, reaching for the consoles. 'As neither of you are
grown up enough to play with each other or with the
computer games, I shall take them away from you and
get the hospital teacher to come in and give you some
extra lessons.'

'What?' cried Liam, aghast.

'No way!' exclaimed Sam, grabbing for the console.
'We've done our lessons for today.'

'Well?' Katherine fixed the pair of them with a stern
gaze. 'I'm not having any more of this nonsense. Frank
has only just come back from his operation. You'll be
disturbing him.' It wasn't strictly true. With the drugs
kicking in, Frank already looked as if the latest heavy
metal band playing next to his ear wouldn't disturb
him.

The two of them glanced across at their sleeping
friend and had the grace to look shamefaced.

'Sorry, Sister,' Sam said quietly.

'If we promise not to argue, can we have the consoles back?' Liam bargained.

Katherine pretended to consider the request.

'All right, then, but only on condition that you don't

argue. The first time I hear raised voices I'll be back to take them away—permanently.'

For the next half-hour she tried to make it obvious that she was keeping her eyes on them, but it was hard. For a start, it seemed as if the phone was going to ring non-stop.

If it wasn't a mix-up over the number of evening meals ordered it was a request for an update on the ward's bed status. Then there were the calls from the friends and families of their young patients, all wanting reassurance and the chance to pass on a message.

It was another hour before a phone call came through, warning her that Laurel was already on her way back to the ward.

'I was expecting her to be in Theatre a lot longer than this,' her mother said as she hovered just out of the way while the porters were settling their charge back into her place in the ward. 'It's such a big operation and on both legs at once.'

'It does make a difference when the patient is otherwise healthy,' Katherine pointed out. 'If Laurel had needed that much surgery after a car crash there would also have had to be all sorts of other things going on at the same time, such as repairs to blood vessels and skin grafts.'

'You mean it would have taken much longer if all that had to be done at once.'

'Exactly. In Laurel's case it was just a straightforward matter of putting a deliberate gap in the bones in her legs then fixing the special frames in position through her skin and into the separated halves of the bones.'

'I'm dreading having to learn how to deal with the frames,' Mrs Kent admitted. 'I'm afraid I won't be able to keep the wires clean enough and she'll get infections. Then there's the matter of having to deliberately inflict pain on my daughter every day as I wind the screws a bit further.'

'Cruel to be kind?' Katherine asked. 'At least you know that Laurel will thank you for it when it's all over.'

'It still seems weird, to deliberately break the bones and then wind the two halves a little further apart every day.'

'It makes sense when you realise that in the space of that day Laurel's body is racing to fill that tiny gap you've created with new bone, just the way it does with an accidental break. Then you wind the halves apart again and off she goes again until eventually she's grown her own extra length of bone to make her taller.'

'You probably think I'm wrong for wanting to put my daughter through all this,' she said suddenly, almost taking Katherine by surprise. 'Some of the members of my husband's family are very angry. They think I'm teaching her to be ashamed of her condition. They think I should be teaching her to accept the way she was born.'

'And what do you think?' Katherine asked, knowing that sometimes a nurse's job was just to act as a sounding-board while patients or their families talked out their concerns.

'I think it's no different than if she was born with any other deformity,' Mrs Kent said decisively. 'If she'd been born with a squint eye or a harelip they wouldn't be faulting me for wanting to have them operated on to make her life a little easier. I don't see that this is any different. It's an operation that has corrected a physical problem for her so she can live a more normal life.'

She glanced down at her daughter and Katherine saw a world of sadness in the woman's eyes.

'If this operation had been possible years ago it might have saved my husband from finally succeeding in committing suicide,' she murmured softly. 'Sometimes, coming to life once a year as one of Snow White's seven friends just isn't enough.'

'Mum?' croaked a little voice in the bed beside them. 'Is it all over yet?'

Instantly the youngster became the focus of their attention but Katherine was glad to know that Mrs Kent was so keen for her daughter to do well.

Apart from the ethics other people adhered to in connection with this sort of operation, there was also the matter of individual choice, and Laurel and her mother were certainly dedicated enough to see the uncomfortable process through.

'Katherine, dear, you're going to need to try the dress on to see if it fits properly,' her mother announced.

The phone had been ringing as she entered the communal area of the staff accommodation block. She'd automatically answered it and been surprised to hear her mother's voice. Knowing what a lottery incoming calls could be, they usually waited for her to ring them.

In the background she could hear her grandmother muttering instructions but she was too busy wondering how she was going to fit in an extra visit home to try to decipher what she was saying. How was she ever going to cope with everything by the time leap year's day arrived?

'How urgently do you need me to come down?' She

was frantically trying to calculate if her next off-duty time would fit in with another quick trip home. She was on an early shift tomorrow, due to finish at about three in the afternoon. That meant that she'd be able to be at her grandmother's by—

'Oh, you don't have to worry about that,' her mother said airily. 'I spoke to Damon at the hospital and he suggested we bring it up to do the fitting at his flat. Then he suggested the four of us could go out together for a meal.'

'Oh, but...' Katherine began, but she may as well not have bothered. Her mother seemed to have developed a remarkable similarity to a bulldozer in the last couple of days.

She'd always admired her mother for the way she'd coped after her divorce, turning a dilettante's interest in jewellery design into a well-respected costume jewellery business. It was funny how that single-minded drive for success seemed so much less attractive when it was turned to organising her daughter's life.

'After all,' her mother continued, blithely unaware of her daughter's scowling expression on the other end of the phone, 'your grandmother and I didn't really have a chance to celebrate your engagement, and if we don't do it soon it'll be too late because you'll already be married.'

The gentle reminder of the speed with which she and Damon were marrying was enough to bring on an instant attack of guilt.

'When were you thinking of coming up?' Katherine asked, resigned to falling in with everyone else's plans.

'Tomorrow afternoon,' her mother said brightly, as if her daughter's agreement was a foregone conclusion. 'Damon's given us his address and directions to the flat in case we need them and suggested that we do the fitting there too. Then we can all go out together afterwards.'

Once again it seemed as if she was going to have no say in the matter and she almost gave a hysterical giggle when she realised that she was now the *only* one who didn't know where her future husband lived.

'About half-past five?' her mother continued. 'That should give us enough time to get to the restaurant by seven, shouldn't it? We don't want to be too late travelling home again afterwards.'

It didn't sound as though she was in much doubt that the dress was already almost perfect, and the more Katherine thought about it the more she got the feeling that she was being manipulated.

If only she'd guessed that this was what her mother would try to do, she could have warned Damon to be on his guard. As it was, they were now condemned to spending almost a whole evening under the eagle eyes of both her relatives.

Ever since Damon had agreed to help her with her plan she had been consumed by the fear that she might unintentionally give the game away. It wasn't until she was lying in bed and thinking about tomorrow's ordeal that she realised that there was something lurking underneath that fear.

Just the thought that the two of them were going to be spending an evening together, pretending to be a blissfully happy engaged couple, filled her with anticipation.

How would Damon cope with it?

Would he treat the situation the way he had when he'd given her his mother's ring? Would he feel that he needed to hold her hand or wrap his arm around her shoulders or, even better, kiss her socks off as he tried to make their audience believe in the make-believe?

The trouble was, *she* already knew that she wouldn't need to act. She'd been trying to suppress her love for Damon for a long time now, and his ready agreement to help her out of her family dilemma had only captivated her more.

In fact, the more she thought about it, the more she wondered why he *had* agreed.

He owed nothing to her or her family and, right from the first, had been open with the fact that he had no intention of marrying.

Still, this was a bone she'd been worrying at for a long time. Now she needed to sleep or she wouldn't be able to work tomorrow. Apart from anything else, she was going to need her wits about her when her mother and grandmother arrived.

'Three admissions during the night. Drugs,' Lenny Price told her as he took her through the usual routine. 'All three are thirteen years old and all in the same class at school. Looks as if there's a bad batch out on the streets so we might be in for some more admissions.'

'How bad are they? Did they have to spend time in Intensive Care before we got them?'

'They seem to have got off with it lightly. Apparently, they'd only taken one dose each and hadn't mixed it with any other drugs or with alcohol. They came straight up here from Accident and Emergency and all three are now fully conscious.'

When Katherine had begun her training, drugs overdoses in such youngsters had been almost unheard of. Now it was a rare week for them not to have children as young as eight or nine admitted with excesses of alcohol or one of the banned substances poisoning their bodies.

'How about Laurel and Frank?' She wasn't supposed to have favourite patients, but sometimes it was difficult not to.

'Laurel and her mum have got everything down to a fine art. When Laurel gives herself a shot of analgesic her mum waits just long enough for her to fall asleep then she disappears into the visitors' lounge to catch up on some sleep. I don't think she's looking forward to learning how to take care of the wounds or turn the screws, but she's going to give it her best shot.'

'How about Frank? Is he finally taking his pain relief often enough?' They sometimes had problems with young male teenagers trying to cope without analgesic after their operations in the mistaken belief that it was macho.

'No problem…once I told him that if he wasn't adult enough to use the self-administered system properly, I'd be giving him a needle in his bum every four hours instead!'

Katherine grinned. 'That's what I like to hear. Attack them where it hurts—in their pride!'

'Mrs Addo gave me the thumbs up, but made sure Frank didn't see!'

The rest was routine and Katherine was already relaxing as concentration on her job allowed her to switch off from her personal concerns when Lenny spoiled it.

'So, when's the wedding going to be?' he demanded, for once apparently not in a hurry to disappear. 'You're a dark horse. How long has all this been going on between you and Dr Damon, the demon lover?'

'Lenny!' she exclaimed.

'Oh, come on! You can't tell me that the two of you haven't been keeping your affair under wraps for months. When did it start? Christmas? Or was it the New Year party?' He gave her a coaxing grin. 'Who would have thought that he had it in him to be so romantic? A Valentine's Day proposal, no less.'

Katherine could only imagine what Lenny would say if he knew that *she* had done the proposing…but that was definitely not for general consumption. It had been hard enough, telling her family.

'You think I'd tell you?' she demanded in scandalised tones. 'You men say that women are gossips but you're the worst of the lot. When Damon and I get married I'll make sure that you're the very last person I tell.'

'You're a cruel woman,' he said in heartbroken tones. 'How am I ever going to hold my head up in the next Gossips Anonymous meeting if I haven't got a single juicy item to share?'

'Go home, Lenny,' she said, flapping her hands at him as though shooing chickens out of a coop. 'Some of us have jobs to do.'

On his way out of the office Lenny paused.

'Hey, Katherine. All joking aside, I'm really pleased for the two of you.' He gave her an awkward hug.

'Unhand my woman!' demanded Damon, and Katherine found herself leaping backwards as though she and Lenny really had something to be guilty about.

Lenny grinned unrepentantly. 'I just thought you'd rather I gave Katherine a congratulatory hug, but if you'd prefer to receive it in person…' He took a couple of steps towards Damon with an evil grin on his face.

'A handshake will be sufficient,' Damon agreed quickly, and they all laughed.

'You make certain you look after her properly,' Lenny warned. 'Our Katherine's special.'

'Don't worry about that. I've known it for a long time,' Damon said softly. His deep blue eyes were fixed on her across the small room as though Lenny had already disappeared.

Her heartbeat stumbled at the expression in his eyes, then it staggered for several slow, heavy beats, before abruptly finding a faster tempo—a much faster tempo.

'Everything organised for tonight?' he asked, his voice sounding strangely husky.

She nodded, unable to find her voice, while it seemed as if her heart was trying to leap up into her throat.

'You don't mind that I invited them to meet us at my flat?' Finally his words penetrated the weird tension that filled the room between them.

'No, I don't mind, except…' She paused, feeling a bit stupid after all these years of knowing him.

'Except…what?' His dark brows drew together into a frown. 'I thought it would be easier to suggest the fitting be done at my flat, rather then trying to find somewhere private enough in the hospital.'

'It's not that. It's… Oh, for heaven's sake, I've no idea where you live.'

Damon was startled into several seconds' silence then he began to laugh.

'Oh, Lord, that would have been a clanger of epic proportions,' he said with a chuckle. 'Here we are, apparently so close that we want to get married immediately, and you don't even know where I live.'

'It's not that funny,' she snapped. 'We've never had that sort of relationship.'

'Hey, little Kat. Claws away,' he said softly, and caught both her hands in his. 'What time does your shift end? I'll give you a lift there so we'll arrive before your family. Then I can give you the quick two-bob tour before they catch you out by asking the way to the bathroom.'

That would solve *some* of their problems but Katherine was certain there were going to be plenty more before this fiasco was over.

Strangely, in spite of the fact that she was prone to pausing in the middle of a task to shudder at the enormity of what they were doing, the rest of her shift went well.

Thank goodness there were no patients scheduled for surgery because they had several admissions for chronic patients experiencing crises.

First in was a twelve-year-old girl in a diabetic coma, followed closely by a fifteen-year-old male asthmatic and a thirteen-year-old young man with thalassaemia.

'Can you tell me what happened, Mrs Griffin?' Katherine asked as she reviewed Tania's file. 'Have you any idea why your daughter's been having so many episodes recently? She's been coping wonderfully ever since she became diabetic at seven. Is she having problems sticking to her diet regimen? Trying to lose weight, perhaps?'

'It's nothing like that, I promise you. She's lucky enough to have a lovely figure without dieting,' Tania's mother said firmly. 'She didn't have any trouble until she was made to change to humulin. It just doesn't seem to give her enough warning before she collapses.'

Katherine took a careful look at the chart that had

begun when Tania had been rushed into Accident and Emergency after her collapse at school. She could see that Tania's temperature and blood pressure had both been abnormally low while her pulse had been very rapid and weak—all signs of insufficient insulin in her system.

She was still rather drowsy and her skin felt too dry, but with the administration of an extra dose of quick-acting insulin downstairs her pulse, temperature and blood pressure were now within normal ranges.

'I expect the endocrinologist will want Tania to stay in for a few days while we have another go at getting her settled,' Katherine warned. 'It's too dangerous to let her go on like this. The more often she goes into a coma, the more likely she is to suffer from eye problems, kidney failure, gangrene or even a stroke.'

Mrs Griffin was clearly horrified. 'At her age? I thought that only happened to older diabetics?'

'Unfortunately, it depends on the degree of damage that occurs rather than the age of the person. Tania will be more at risk with every one of these episodes.'

Katherine was pleased that the endocrinologist on duty was someone that Mrs Griffin obviously recognised, and she left the two of them conferring seriously while they waited for Tania to recover sufficiently to join in the conversation.

Doubtless, their conclusions would be passed on in the form of requests for changes in her drug regimen while they tried to get her stabilised.

Ian Longrigg was a patient with an alarmingly bulky file for someone only fifteen years old, but as a lifelong asthmatic he'd obviously suffered more than his fair share of serious attacks.

Katherine had already seen him on Windermere

Ward once before and had grown to like the quiet, studious boy. She could hear his wheezy breathing right across the ward, in spite of the mask covering his face and the sound of the nebuliser helping to deliver the bronchodilating drugs.

'Hello, Ian. Couldn't wait to visit Windy Ward again?' she teased, and received a tired grin for her pains. 'Any idea what set you off this time?'

They'd never discovered what had triggered his last couple of episodes, which made it difficult to prevent it happening again.

She knew he would have been asked the same question when he arrived, so she was startled to see him nodding and beckoning her.

'Dissection,' he whispered hoarsely and choked for several seconds before he caught his breath again. 'Biology practical.'

Katherine remembered those classes from her own schooldays all too well. 'Fur and formalin,' she said with a grimace, and received a thumbs up from Ian.

The trouble was, it was all very well knowing what was triggering his most recent attacks. It would make preventing a recurrence fairly easy if he just avoided the situation. But what would it do to the youngster's dream of being a doctor?

In most cases it was fairly simple to administer drugs to counteract the life-threatening spasms in his bronchial tubes, but the possibility of coping with such severe attacks on a daily basis was not an option.

As she moved on to the third of their new patients she wondered whether Damon could find out what provision medical schools had in place for such candidates. Surely the fact that Ian had suffered from asthma all his life should make him a more sympathetic doctor, rather than bar him from joining the profession.

Paolo Serapiglia looked closer to ten or eleven years old rather than the thirteen indicated on his case notes.

His thalassaemia had been diagnosed from a blood sample soon after he was born and he had been undergoing treatment to combat the effects of the genetically transmitted disease ever since.

Apart from regular treatment with penicillin to combat his susceptibility to infection, today he would probably have to receive as much as five hundred millilitres of washed, packed red cells and chelation therapy to reduce the toxic side effects of excess iron.

'How's the pain in your joints now, Paolo?' Katherine asked, pleased to see that his eyes were much brighter than they had been when he'd first been brought onto the ward.

'It's not so bad,' he said stoically, then flashed her a wicked grin. 'It was my own fault for running after the pretty girls, but I thought it would make a different part of me ache, not my knees and hips and ankles. You wouldn't run away so fast, would you?'

'Hey, Casanova, leave my girl alone,' said a familiar voice, and Katherine whirled to find Damon standing behind her with a similarly wicked grin on his face.

CHAPTER FIVE

'IT'S such a shame,' Katherine said suddenly, trying to break the uncomfortable silence that had begun to fill the car like an invisible presence between them.

'What is?' Damon clearly had no idea of the direction her train of thought had taken.

'Paolo's illness. He's such a chirpy lad that it doesn't seem fair for him to spend so much of his time in hospital.'

'It's better than the alternative,' Damon pointed out quietly. 'It's not many years ago that someone so severely affected by thalassaemia could have died before he even reached school age. Paolo has already reached his teens and, barring any major complications or bouts of infection, might even survive into his twenties or thirties.'

'If you put it like that...' Katherine had to agree that it was better than the alternative. In a family of three boys, all having inherited thalassaemia from their carrier parents, Paolo was certainly faring better than either of his brothers. For the most part he seemed to manage to keep his health on a fairly even keel—when he wasn't chasing the girls.

'Have you heard any more from your mother?' Damon asked, and immediately she felt herself grow tense with apprehension.

'Nothing since her call yesterday, but I can't decide whether that's a good thing or a bad one.'

He chuckled. 'Don't worry about it. It'll all work out

all right. I'll ply them with alcohol as soon as they step inside the door and soon they'll be too cross-eyed to see us, never mind ask us pointed questions.'

Katherine had to chuckle, too. The mental image of her mother and grandmother propping each other up while Damon topped up their glasses was irresistible.

'I hope you've got some Dutch courage for me, too,' she said darkly. 'If it all goes wrong tonight there won't be time to do anything about it. There are less than ten days to go.'

Damon's flat was in one of the more modern blocks with private parking facilities in an underground car park, and he'd already arranged for her mother to be admitted to one of the visitors' slots when she arrived.

By the time the two of them reached his front door there was only half an hour before her family was due to arrive and Katherine was visibly trembling.

Damon tried to hand her the overnight bag in which she'd carried her off-duty clothing to the hospital that morning, but she fumbled so badly that it fell to the floor with a thud.

'Hey, Katherine, calm down,' he soothed, and to her surprise he wrapped both arms around her and pulled her towards him until she was resting against the much-needed strength of his body. 'It'll be all right,' he murmured softly as one hand stroked rhythmically up and down her back. 'We'll be all right. Trust me.'

'Is that "Trust me, I'm a doctor" or "Trust me, I'm a man"?' she demanded through chattering teeth.

'It's "Trust me, I'm your friend",' he corrected, tightening his arms around her briefly before he released her. 'Now, are you ready for the two-bob tour? Then it'll be time for you to take your uniform off.'

'What...?' The thought of taking her clothes off in

Damon's flat when they were alone together was blowing fuses inside her head. 'Why?'

'Several reasons,' he said calmly as he led the way along the corridor. 'Bathroom and toilet in there. Shower unit over the bath. Previous tenant left a shower curtain printed with sharks.'

He pushed the door open and flicked on the light to give her a quick glimpse. The thought of the eminently grown-up Dr Cade taking a shower behind all those cartoons of man-eating sharks made her want to giggle.

'As I said, they weren't my choice but I haven't bothered to change it because it does the job quite adequately.'

She deliberately caught his eye and they both laughed.

'Well, at least that stopped you looking as if you expected me to murder you at any minute,' he said with a smug expression on his face. 'This is the spare room-cum-study and is a complete mess…as you can see.'

Once again he pushed the door open so that she could see inside the room.

'It's chaos!' she exclaimed when she saw the serried ranks of packing cases stacked against one wall and the desk and bookshelves filling the opposite one.

'Is there actually room for you to sit on your chair when you pull it out from under the desk?' she asked. 'What on earth *is* all that stuff? You're obviously not using any of it, so if it's rubbish why don't you just get rid of it?'

Damon was silent for a long moment and she began to wonder if he'd been insulted by her suggestion. She was just about to apologise when he spoke.

'Actually, I don't really know what's in the boxes,' he admitted quietly. 'They're my brother's belongings, some of them left over from his time in the forces, and I haven't been able to make myself go through them yet.'

'Oh, Damon, I'm so sorry,' she gasped, backing out of the room as fast as she could. 'That was so thoughtless of me. I never would have—'

'Hey, Katherine, it's all right. You weren't to know,' he said soothingly as he switched off the light and pulled the door firmly shut. 'Anyway, you're quite right about it. It's time I sorted it all out and got rid of the rubbish. For all I know there are the whole contents of Damian's larder carefully stacked somewhere in that room, mutating into alien life forms.'

Once more he'd managed to find a way of lightening the atmosphere but Katherine felt dreadful that it had been necessary. Perhaps if she kept her mouth closed she would avoid saying anything dreadful.

'This is my room,' he announced, and this time walked all the way in, obviously expecting her to follow. 'As I said before, I'd suggest that you take your uniform off before your family arrives and leave it on the bed. There's my towelling dressing-gown hanging on the back of the door for you to put on.'

'But…' She had to swallow and try again. 'You suggested that before, but why don't I wait until they arrive before I take it off? Then I wouldn't have to borrow your dressing-gown. I could just go straight from trying the dress on to getting ready to go out.'

'Ah, but it's all a matter of appearances. If you're wearing my dressing-gown it will make your mother and grandmother think that you're a frequent enough visitor here to be able to make free with my belongings. Likewise the fact that you feel comfortable enough to leave your uniform lying on my bed. Once they see the

state of the spare room they'll automatically think that
when you come here we share my room.'

'Oh, but—'

'And that's exactly what we *want* them to think, Kat.
Having what they think is "evidence" put right in front
of them will surprise them so much that it'll stop them
asking the obvious questions.'

It made a strange sort of sense when he put it that
way, although she didn't hold out much hope for her
grandmother remaining startled for long.

'Just the living room and kitchen to go,' he announced, and led the way, leaving the light on in his
bedroom.

The living room was surprisingly spacious and had
large windows on two adjoining walls.

'What sort of view have you got from up here?' She
peered out into the February darkness, but apart from
some rows of streetlights set between leafless trees everything seemed strangely dark.

'That's the best part about this end of the block,' he
said, and she found herself watching his reflection in
the window as he came to stand behind her.

She held her breath, waiting to feel the first point of
contact between them as he continued speaking, apparently oblivious of her distraction.

'I've got a view of a small park out of this side and
the edge of the hospital grounds out of the other. It
almost makes it seem as if I'm looking out on my own
private stately acres without having to do anything
about the upkeep.'

In spite of the space he seemed to be maintaining
between the two of them she could almost feel the heat
radiating from his body.

For two years she'd managed to keep her attraction

towards him under control, but ever since she'd had the crazy idea of proposing to him it had been as if she'd relinquished that control.

It took a real effort to force her mind back to their conversation and she took a step away before she turned to face him.

'Grandmother will be envious. She's always complaining that she has to wage a constant war with her gardener to get him to do what she wants. Mind you, Tom's been with her for nearly twenty years so I think it's more a case of enjoying the battles than resenting each other for them.'

Katherine was smiling at the memories of some of the arguments when she caught sight of Damon checking the time on his watch.

'Oh, God,' she muttered, brought back to the present with a bump. 'How long till they're due?'

'Long enough for you to stick your head in my kitchen. It's hardly bigger than a broom cupboard but it's big enough for a bachelor's requirements.'

'Especially when he can use the canteen at work to save him having to cook for himself,' she teased, then stuck her head through the narrow archway in one wall of the sitting room. 'Anyway, it's not *that* small. I'd have described it as compact. You've got all the essentials here, including a full-sized cooker and a microwave.'

'I bow to your greater expertise,' he said with a salute. 'Now I'm going to put the kettle on while you run away and get undressed.'

Katherine wished he hadn't used those words. They conjured up far too many images inside her head as she stripped off her tunic top and trousers. She was about to fold them neatly and leave them in a pile on the corner of Damon's bed when she caught herself.

'Mother would never believe I'm accustomed to being in this room if I folded anything neatly,' she muttered, and draped both items of clothing haphazardly to dangle towards the oatmeal-coloured carpet. 'That looks far more my style...unfortunately.'

All too aware that Damon could want to enter his room at any moment she swiftly grabbed his dressing-gown. She slid her arms into the sleeves and started to wrap the thick fabric around her waist when she suddenly froze then drew in a deep breath.

Why hadn't she realised that if this was Damon's dressing-gown it would smell like him? With all these yards of fabric surrounding her it was almost as if Damon himself was wrapped around her.

A sharp rap at the door brought her to her senses and she hurriedly tightened the belt.

'Cup of tea ready as soon as you are,' Damon called.

'I...I'm decent. You can come in,' she called back. 'Do you need to change your clothes before we go out? You won't have much chance if the three of us are in here, playing with hemlines and suchlike.'

'Good thinking,' he agreed as he pushed the door open and advanced to hand her a cup of tea.

The cup rattled in the saucer as Katherine took hold of it so she hurriedly lifted it to take a tiny sip.

She hadn't even realised that her eyes were following Damon across the room to put his own tea on top of the chest of drawers until she saw him strip his tie away with one well-practised tug and then start undoing his shirt buttons.

With the cup poised halfway between the saucer and her open mouth she froze, fascinated and horrified at the same time when she realised that he was actually undressing in front of her.

She didn't know she'd made a sound but he must have heard something because when her eyes travelled up the broad swathe of naked skin as far as his face she found him watching her just as closely.

'I—I'd better go and wait in the sitting room,' she stammered, the cup crashing down when her cheeks suddenly blazed with embarrassment. She lifted it to her mouth again in a desperate attempt to hide her face. How on earth was she going to get out of here with any semblance of dignity?

'You don't have to go for *my* sake,' he said wickedly. 'I've often wondered what the attraction was for men to join these strip-tease groups. I think I've just found out.'

'And?' she asked with an attempt at nonchalance that probably fell far short of believable. Were her eyes really standing out as far as they felt?

'I've discovered that if a man watches the expression on a woman's face when he's taking off his clothes and finds approval there, it does wonders for his ego,' Damon said huskily.

All the time they'd been talking he'd continued to release the tiny buttons one by one, finally reaching the cuffs. As Katherine watched he shrugged sharply so that the white cotton slid away to fall in a heap on the floor behind him.

He was much broader than she'd expected, at least a yard and a half, she thought as her eyes followed the curved perfection of the muscles delineating his chest and abdomen. The dark swirls of hair stretching from one flat male nipple to the other emphasised the width still further and provided a perfect contrast to the narrowness of his waist and hips.

His hands moved to the waistband of his suit trousers, the charcoal grey fabric still carrying a clear crease down the front of each leg even at the end of a long day.

As she watched he grew still without beginning to undo them.

'Kat?'

The strangely husky sound of his own personal nickname for her drew her eyes up to meet his.

'Hmm?' She wondered why he'd stopped. She'd been looking forward to seeing whether the rest of his body was as perfect as what she'd seen already.

'Kat!' Damon's voice was sharper this time, and to her shock she suddenly realised that she'd been standing there blatantly ogling him while he prepared to take the rest of his clothes off.

'Oh, God! I'm so sorry,' she apologised, whirling away from him and nearly falling over the corner of the bed in her haste to get out of the room. Thank goodness her cup was empty or she'd have spilled the lot.

'Kat, wait! You don't understand,' he was calling as she sped out of the door into the welcome dimness of the unlit corridor. 'The bell,' Damon said, his voice coming closer again, and she turned towards the sound like a hunted animal hearing danger. The cup and saucer were clenched in either hand as though she was contemplating using them as a shield...or a weapon, perhaps?

'Kat, I heard the bell,' he called, suddenly coming to a halt in the doorway when he realised she was still only a few feet away, almost cowering against the wall.

'Kat,' he said softly, as though still afraid that she was going to bolt away from him. 'I've got an admission to make. If it weren't for the fact that your mother and your grandmother are waiting outside my front door I would have been perfectly willing to strip off every inch of clothing while you watched—except I've never done a strip-tease in my life and I don't know who would have been more embarrassed...you or me.'

The doorbell rang again, breaking into his startling admission almost like a punctuation mark, and they both glanced distractedly towards the sound.

'Will you let them in for me?' he asked softly, a wry grin lifting one corner of his mouth. 'Only you're wearing my dressing-gown and it's going to take either a very cold shower or a lot more minutes than I want to leave them waiting out there before I'll have calmed down enough to greet them.'

Katherine wasn't certain what he was talking about until he started to turn away and she saw the light in his bedroom fall across the front of his trousers.

Her face still felt as if it was on fire when she released the latch and swung the front door open, having deposited the cup and saucer on the way.

'Darling, you're here already. When no one came to answer the door I wondered if we'd arrived too soon,' her mother said as she stepped into the narrow hallway. 'Sorry, I haven't got any hands free or I'd give you a hug.'

'If I relieved you of your burden, then you could,' Katherine pointed out, grateful for the change of mood. She would only need a couple of minutes of her mother's brand of chatter before she had herself under control again.

She reached out to take the hanger out of her

mother's hand, careful not to squash the vast swathe
of rustling plastic that covered the precious dress.

'I could take it straight through,' her mother offered,
and Katherine nearly choked.

'Um, I'm not certain whether... Uh, Damon was just
going to get his clothes on...I mean, change his clothes
before we take over the bedroom for the fitting.'

She'd thought her face had been red when she'd realised that Damon had become aroused watching her
watching him. That was nothing to the heat radiating
from her cheeks when she realised what the two older
women were thinking.

Both her mother and her grandmother had put together the fact that she was wearing Damon's dressing-
gown with her certain knowledge that he was in his
room putting on some clothes, and had obviously come
up with an interrupted romantic interlude.

She didn't know whether to be annoyed that Damon
had been absolutely right in his assessment of their
reactions, to be grateful that family antennae had been
successfully misdirected or to be disappointed that,
apart from watching him take his shirt off, absolutely
nothing had happened.

'In that case, perhaps you'd better be the one to carry
the dress through,' her mother conceded archly.

Unfortunately for Katherine's peace of mind, her
parent wasn't the only one obviously fighting to con-
ceal a grin, and she was only too glad to turn her back
on the two of them to stalk along the corridor towards
the other end of the flat.

'If you'd like to shut the front door, the sitting room
is along this way too,' she informed them loftily, hoping she didn't look too much like a scared rabbit running away.

'What on earth is happening to me?' she demanded
on a groan as she flung herself through Damon's bedroom door and hastily shut it behind her, barely whisk-
ing the dress through in time. 'I'm a nurse—a respon-
sible, professional woman—not a brainless ninny.'

'Problem?' Damon asked as he stepped closer to re-
lieve her of her burden.

For several seconds she was silent, taking in the
sight that met her very appreciative eyes.

Instead of his usual classic grey suits, teamed with
equally classic shirts and ties, he had changed into a
pair of black pleated trousers. His shirt had a narrow
band instead of a collar and looked almost blindingly
white against a supple black leather jacket.

He looked totally, utterly delicious and she couldn't
take her eyes off him, especially when he was just
inches away from her…close enough to reach out and
see if the leather of his jacket was as smooth as it
looked and the fabric of his shirt as silky soft.

'Uh, Kat?' Damon stopped to clear his throat and
she suddenly noticed that the skin over his cheekbones
had taken on a darker hue. Had he actually been embarrassed by the way she was looking at his clothes?
He hadn't even been taking them off this time, so—

'Kat, what was the problem with your family?' he
said again, turning away to hang the dress on the front
edge of his wardrobe door.

She suddenly remembered why she'd come rushing
into his room without so much as a knock on the door.

'You were right, of course,' she said, flinging her
arms out for emphasis. 'I went to the door wearing this
and when my mother suggested that she should carry
that wretched dress through to your room I suddenly

thought you might still be, well, not quite ready for visitors.'

'Certainly not ready to entertain my future mother-in-law,' he agreed with a wicked grin.

'Of course, when I tried to explain that, the two of them thought they'd interrupted us while we were...' She gestured towards the bed, determined not to have to find the words.

She could have killed Damon when he began to laugh. In fact, she'd curled both hands into fists and was advancing on him with mayhem in mind.

'Now, then, Kat, don't do anything you might live to regret,' he said through his chuckles, stepping back just far enough to stay out of range.

'That's just the trouble,' she muttered through clenched teeth. 'Just lately it seems as if I'm going to live to regret *everything* I'm doing—but that's no reason why I should let *you* live.'

She launched a sudden attack but where she expected to meet resistance she found none. Instead of trying to combat the charge, Damon accepted it, wrapping his arms around her as he began to fall over backwards.

It wasn't until she found herself spread out across his chest after a much softer landing than she'd expected that she realised they'd come to rest in the middle of his bed.

'Well, now that you've got me here, what are you going to do with me?' he demanded wickedly.

Suddenly aware of every virile inch of him, Katherine could think of any number of things she'd like to do with him, starting with—

'Katherine, dear, are you nearly ready to try—? Oh, my word!'

The sound of her mother's hasty retreat from the bedroom door was almost as embarrassing as being caught spread-eagled across Damon's body.

'Oh, my God!' she wailed, but when she tried to roll away from him he tightened his grip around her waist and effortlessly kept her in place. 'Damon, let me go. Oh, this is terrible. What must she be thinking of us?'

'Exactly what you wanted her to think…what *we* wanted her to think,' he corrected himself. 'This couldn't have worked out better if we'd tried to stage it deliberately.'

'What do you…? Oh!' The penny dropped.

She'd been so worried about presenting the right impression that she'd forgotten that actions could speak louder than words. Afraid that her grandmother and mother would guess that her marriage to Damon had only been arranged to save them from losing their home, she'd ignored the fact that it wasn't just a case of saying the right words.

Breathing out a huge sigh, she allowed herself to relax, her head coming to rest somewhere just over Damon's heart. For several long seconds she lay listening to the powerful beat and found the steady rhythm utterly soothing.

'Ready to face them, yet?' he prompted, his voice reaching her through the wall of his chest as much as from his mouth.

'Not in this lifetime,' she groaned. 'I'm already blushing so much you'll be able to use the heat to make toast.'

He was chuckling as he helped her to sit up.

'Would it help if you only had to deal with one of them? I could entertain your grandmother while you and your mother deal with pins and measurements.'

In spite of her fears, the rest of the evening went well.

Not once did her mother refer to what she'd seen when she'd opened Damon's bedroom door, and she was almost certain from her grandmother's calm composure that she hadn't been told anything about it.

The dress had fitted perfectly, confirming Katherine's suspicion that the trip had been a ruse to watch the two of them together.

'It's time for us to make our way home,' her mother said as soon as Damon brought them back to his flat after dinner. 'We'll come up in plenty of time to help you get ready for the ceremony—unless you'd rather have one of your friends with you?'

There was such a hopeful note in her mother's voice that Katherine couldn't deny her.

'As the ceremony's going to be in the hospital chapel it makes sense for me to get dressed there. I think Damon's going to have his car parked nearby to take us for a meal afterwards.'

'And then we're going to go to our hotel while you travel home,' her mother finished. 'In a way it's a pity that getting married at such short notice is stopping you from having a proper honeymoon.'

'Still, we can always do that later,' Katherine said dismissively, avoiding her mother's eyes in case her guilt was written large in her own.

Hopefully, by the time anyone brought up the question of the missing honeymoon again, the will would have finished passing from one solicitor's hand to another and her grandmother could stop worrying about having to sell her home. Then she and Damon would be free to concoct a reason why they were ending their marriage. The saying 'Marry in haste, repent at leisure' should fit the bill admirably.

'Don't forget, if you need any help with any-thing...?' her grandmother offered as she gave Katherine a last hug.

'You've done so much for me all my life,' Katherine murmured as she gently held the older woman. In spite of her grandfather's feud with her mother, her grand-mother had never once forgotten her birthday or Christmas and had always been ready with a listening ear.

Guilt nearly swamped her when she realised that al-most every word of their last two meetings had been lies and she briefly tightened her arms.

Her grandmother squeaked a protest that she was being squeezed to death and Katherine suddenly real-ised how prominent the elderly lady's ribs were. She knew that losing her husband had aged her but she hadn't noticed just how fragile she'd become these days.

With that realisation came the determination that she and Damon were doing the right thing. It was bad enough that her grandmother had become a widow, but if there was any way to avoid it she wasn't going to lose her beloved home as well.

'What you can do for me is make sure that Mum doesn't buy one of those enormous hats to wear to the wedding,' Katherine said with a slightly wobbly smile. 'I've never been able to convince her that short peo-ple just look like walking mushrooms if their hats are too big.'

CHAPTER SIX

KATHERINE'S eyes took another swift trip around the hospital chapel, almost as if she was looking for an escape route.

It was a plain and simple room with pale painted walls and pale honey-coloured wooden pews to complement the single arched, stained-glass window behind the unadorned altar.

Usually the atmosphere in here was peaceful, somewhere where tormented patients, family or friends could come to pray or just to seek solitude for a little while.

Today, much to her amazement, it was full.

Behind her she could hear the rustles and murmurs of dozens of members of staff, some dressed in their finery while others, still in uniform, had obviously snatched time away from their shifts to be with them.

'Do you, Katherine Gillard, take Damon Cade…?'

The time-honoured words had been flowing around her like some strange mist, cutting her off from her surroundings until that moment.

Her hands tightened reflexively over the stem of the single perfect blood-red rose Damon had handed her when she'd joined him at the front of the chapel.

She'd barely glanced in his direction, so wrapped up had she been in the thoughts inside her head. Suddenly she turned and looked straight at him.

For a moment she was disappointed to see that he was wearing a dark suit, half wishing that he'd chosen

YOURS FREE!

One more thing – when you accept the FREE books you could also receive this stunning Starfish Necklace. Crafted with a goldtone finish, this beautiful pendant is a lovely piece to add to your jewellery collection.

CLAIM CHART		
7	7	7	**WORTH *4 FREE* Books plus a Necklace**
🍒	🍒	🍒	**WORTH *3 FREE* Books plus a Necklace**
🔔	🔔	🔔	**WORTH *2 FREE* Books**

YES! I have scratched away the three silver panels above. Please send me all the FREE gifts for which I qualify. I understand that I am under no obligation to purchase any books as explained on the opposite page and overleaf. I am over 18 years of age.

M0BI

MS/MRS/MISS/MR _____ INITIALS _____

BLOCK CAPITALS PLEASE

SURNAME _____

ADDRESS _____

_____

POSTCODE _____

MILLS & BOON READER SERVICE™
FREE BOOK OFFER
FREEPOST CN81
CROYDON
SURREY
CR9 3WZ

NO
STAMP
NEEDED IF
POSTED IN
THE UK
OR N.I.

to wear the collar-less shirt and leather jacket he'd worn when they'd taken her family out for a meal. Somehow it had hinted at a less obviously professional—a slightly wilder—side to his nature.

As if he'd been waiting for her to look at him he met her gaze, and in that moment everything became crystal clear.

She loved Damon Cade.

She'd loved him for the past two years—therefore any promises she made today were nothing more than the plain, honest truth.

'I do,' she said softly but clearly, knowing that if he cared to look he would see the truth of it in her eyes.

With the heavy weight of guilt removed her heart felt light enough to float, and she didn't even try to stop the happy smile that crept over her face as the ceremony drew to a close.

'You may kiss your bride,' said the chaplain with a beaming smile of his own. Poor man, Katherine thought fleetingly. He probably didn't have many opportunities for conducting the happier services of his profession.

Then Damon took her in his arms and tilted his head towards hers and she stopped thinking altogether.

It had been nearly a week since the two of them had managed to snatch any time together and she'd been wondering frantically whether she'd imagined the electricity between them.

The first contact between their lips told her that her imagination hadn't done the sensation justice. This was nuclear meltdown, and as she dissolved against him she had no idea whether it had affected her brain or her knees first.

All she knew was that this was worth every minute

of the worry she'd gone through over the last eleven days since she'd decided on her mad leap year's proposal.

'That's enough,' Katherine heard her grandmother hiss over the sound of appreciative chuckles, and she started to giggle when she heard her add indignantly, 'Well, this *is* a house of God, you know.'

'To be continued later?' Katherine suggested with a happy grin as she and Damon turned to face the congregation.

They had started to make their way out into the corridor when they were surrounded by a laughing group of colleagues and swept off in the opposite direction to the car park exit.

'Hold tight,' Damon muttered as he wrapped a steadying arm around her. 'What are you idiots up to?' he demanded.

'Is my grandmother all right? She won't get knocked off her feet, will she?' Katherine fretted.

Damon stole a hasty look over his shoulder and turned back with a frown on his face.

'She and your mother look as if they're being escorted like royalty. We're the only ones being treated like flotsam.'

As he spoke they were suddenly rushed through a nearby door to be met with a chorus of congratulations.

'Is there *anybody* left on duty in this hospital?' he asked, clearly bemused by the whole thing.

'Well, we weren't going to be cheated out of an excuse to celebrate,' Lenny Price declared. 'We couldn't all fit in the chapel so we thought this was the next best thing.' He gestured towards the other end of the room, and for the first time Katherine noticed their names on the hand-written banner draped across the

wall and the row of tables groaning under a mountain
of food.

'My word! I never expected anything like this!'
Katherine heard her grandmother exclaim and turned
just in time to see her catch sight of the pièce de rés-
istance.

In pride of place in the centre was a magnificent
three-tiered cake in all its gleaming white splendour.

'Didn't we do well?' Shari demanded with a very
self-satisfied grin on her face.

'But how...?' Katherine gestured weakly as the
room continued to fill. 'It was going to be just a quiet
early afternoon wedding with a meal afterwards at a
local hotel.'

Damon caught her elbow and gestured towards
Louise, Fran and Lenny, now huddled together with
her mother and grandmother.

'They certainly don't look as if they've just been
introduced,' he said darkly. 'I think we've been set up.'

'Do you mind?' she asked softly, watching her
grandmother flirt with Lenny as saucily as any of the
1920s flappers.

'Actually, it's rather a compliment that they wanted
to do it,' he returned, then chuckled. 'I suppose we
could see it as getting our just deserts. Your family
pulling the wool over our eyes about the reception
while we're fooling them about the reason for the wedding.'

Damon's reminder of the objective of the whole
event could have put a damper on it for her, but all it
did was spur her into fresh resolve.

She might have proposed this marriage as a way of
helping her family to keep their home, but along the
way she'd had to admit that there was nothing she

would like more than for this bogus marriage to become real.

She knew from Damon's reaction to her that he wasn't immune to the sexual attraction between them. Was it possible that she would be able to build on that attraction until he discovered that he was in love with her, too?

'A toast to the happy couple,' announced Lenny over an hour later when hefty inroads had been made into the mountain of food.

He seemed to have appointed himself the unofficial master of ceremonies but nobody was complaining as they grabbed glasses and passed bottles around.

Because many of the staff present were either on duty or on call the drinks over the last hour had been limited to non-alcoholic. When she saw the label on the champagne bottle Katherine realised that this one was going to be the exception.

'I give you Katherine and Damon—the bride and groom,' Lenny announced with a flourish worthy of an old-time music hall.

'The bride and groom,' echoed the rest of their guests with a cheer. It might not have been the standard format for a wedding reception but everyone was obviously enjoying themselves too much to care.

'Time to cut the cake,' Lenny announced. 'Is there a surgeon in the room or shall we trust Damon to make the first incision?'

Amid laughter, the two of them were ushered forward to the cake, now standing in splendid isolation in the middle of a table.

Damon placed his hand over hers on the knife, and

to the accompaniment of a barrage of camera flashes they symbolically made the first cut together.

'Three tiers!' Damon muttered. 'When did anyone have time to prepare all this?'

'According to some of the gossip around the room, some of our colleagues have got unexpected sidelines outside the hospital.'

Suddenly she remembered other snippets of conversation she'd accidentally overheard on the ward during the last week. They all made sense now.

'Damon, do you think we'd be able to get someone to send some of the cake up to Windy Ward? I've got a feeling that some of the patients already know a fair bit about this and they're having to miss out on the event itself.'

'Now that I think about it, Frank *has* seemed particularly smug about something,' he agreed. 'No doubt he's already got Lenny detailed to bring the leftovers up to the ward.'

'What time are the two of you thinking of leaving?' her mother asked, her cheeks quite pink with all the excitement. Even her grandmother appeared to have taken on a new lease of life, surrounded by an entourage of young men who seemed to be hanging on her every word.

Damon glanced at his watch and Katherine saw his eyebrows lift in surprise.

'I hadn't realised that we'd been here so long,' he admitted. 'I suppose, with one lot returning to work and the next lot arriving, we've had a constantly changing cast of friends around us and just haven't noticed the time passing.'

'You don't want to be too late getting to your hotel,

either,' Katherine pointed out. 'I suppose if we leave, everyone else will start to drift away, too.'

'I expect the die-hards will stay to polish off the remains of the food—and the drink—but that doesn't mean we can't leave,' Damon agreed. 'At least we won't have the rest of the traditions to go through, such as the throwing of the bouquet.'

Katherine tightened her hand on the stem of her rose, almost as if defying anyone to wrest it from her. She had every intention of pressing it between the pages of the family bible. Then, if her hope that their marriage would last didn't materialise, she would always have the rose he'd given her as a memento.

They'd hoped to be able to slip away fairly quietly, but they'd reckoned without Lenny's sharp eyes.

Instead of a dignified retreat it became something akin to hue and cry as they were boisterously escorted towards Damon's car.

'What the…!' he exclaimed when he caught sight of it for the first time.

Every inch seemed to be either covered with enormous red hearts and bows or had bunches of balloons tied to it.

'Uh-uh! Not allowed!' Lenny warned with a wagging finger when Damon would have untied the strings on the driver's door. 'And we're going to escort you for the first few miles to make sure you don't take anything off.'

Katherine's groan echoed Damon's.

'Let's get it over with,' he muttered and pressed the electronic gadget on his key ring to open the locks. 'At least the luggage was locked in the car so they won't have been able to interfere with that.'

He helped her into the passenger seat, carefully making sure that the precious dress was out of the way of the door.

While she watched Damon circle the bonnet to get in the other side she remembered her grandmother saying she couldn't wait to put the two photographs side by side on the piano—the first one of herself in the dress all those years ago and the second one of her granddaughter, wearing the same dress.

'I hope your marriage will be every bit as happy as ours was,' she'd whispered as she'd hugged Katherine. 'Remember, men don't usually know what they really want until we women tell them.'

Katherine had been torn between guilt and laughter. At least she would do her best to take her grandmother's advice. If she could persuade Damon that what he really wanted was to stay married to her, then they might end up as happy as her grandparents had been.

'Thank goodness that journey's over,' Damon said with a heartfelt sigh as they drew up outside the front of the house. 'I thought they were going to follow us all the way here to make sure we didn't take the decorations off.'

In the end they'd been worried that the police might view the car as a driving hazard and had pulled into a hotel car park on the pretext of needing to use the bathroom. Their unofficial escort had pulled in too and had sat in their car, watching their prey.

It had been embarrassing going into the hotel lounge in her wedding dress and it had taken determination to stay there while they were obviously the sole topic of conversation.

Nevertheless, they'd outwaited their tormentors and

had made the rest of the journey with the back seat of the car totally filled with the extravagant decorations.

'At least we know the house will be all right,' Katherine said. 'If we'd intended staying at a hotel for the night I wouldn't have put it past Lenny to find out which one and do something similar with the room.'

She waited while Damon unlocked the front door but when she would have stepped inside he caught her by the elbow and stopped her.

'At least this is one tradition we can follow,' he said as he bent to sweep her up in his arms.

Katherine gave a startled shriek and flung her arm around his neck.

Not that she was afraid that he would drop her. She had a feeling that she'd never been safer than she was at this moment.

'Ready?' he asked as he tightened his arms around her then stepped over the threshold.

She expected him to put her down but he stood in the gloom of the hallway, without making any attempt to lower her feet to the floor.

'Damon? Is something wrong?' she prompted. The house around them was quite silent so he couldn't be listening for intruders.

Her voice echoed slightly and seemed to stir him into action.

'No. Nothing's wrong,' he said as he slowly allowed her to slide to the floor. 'I was just thinking… Oh, it doesn't matter,' he finished dismissively. 'Do you know where the nearest light switch is?'

Katherine had a strange feeling that whatever he'd been thinking might have been very important indeed, but he'd obviously decided not to tell her. Perhaps later, when they'd had time to settle in, he would feel more like talking.

Katherine found the switch and the hallway was filled with a warm buttery glow. She turned to Damon, about to suggest that they go into the kitchen to decide what to eat. There was a special warmth growing inside her at the thought of preparing their first meal together when he began to walk away from her.

'If you're all right here, I'll go and bring the luggage in,' he offered briskly, and before she could utter a word he'd disappeared into the darkness.

'Obviously, I'll be getting the meal, then,' she said wryly, and couldn't help hearing the slightly forlorn tone as her voice echoed back to her.

Damon paused in the darkness beyond the square of light spilling out onto the driveway and turned to lean on the car.

It was so quiet here, after the non-stop noise of massed humanity surrounding the hospital. The only sounds he could hear were the various clicks and ticks as the engine cooled down after the journey, but that was good enough. He desperately needed a few minutes to get his head together.

He'd nearly lost it when he'd stood in the darkness with Kat in his arms. All he'd been able to think of doing was finding the nearest bedroom and getting her out of that dress.

Then she'd spoken and he'd suddenly remembered what was really going on here.

This wasn't the first night of his honeymoon, much as it might seem so to the serried ranks of friends and colleagues they'd left at the hospital. His own body had begun believing it, too, when she'd wrapped her arm around his neck and clung to him like that.

It wasn't until he'd heard her voice that he'd remembered that she'd asked him to enter into this bogus marriage purely to save her family from losing their home.

Kat regarded him as her friend and had turned to that friend for help. How could he even be thinking about betraying her trust for his own physical gratification? Had he no honour?

When they'd first met, two years ago, he'd told her that he never intended marrying, and she'd espoused the same ideal. It was only her own family's dire circumstances that had forced her to go back on her words, not a change in her convictions. She wasn't to know that in the last two years he'd had a change of heart and now bitterly regretted his adamant stance.

He'd like nothing better now than to be able to go into the house and carry Kat off to the nearest flat surface. The only bar to the length of time he wanted to spend making love to her would be the return of her family in two days' time, but even that would only signal a pause while they transferred themselves to his flat.

His attraction towards her had been growing slowly and steadily for so long now that sometimes he couldn't remember a time when he hadn't desired her. Sharing this house with her for the next two days, that was going to be his own private version of hell if he was to keep his raging urges under control.

At least with her mother and grandmother out of the house they weren't going to have to keep up the pretence of being starry-eyed honeymooners. If they'd had to share a bed for the next two nights, her barely clad body just inches away from his, he didn't think he'd have stood a chance of resisting the temptation.

*   *   *

'I suppose we'd better think about taking our luggage upstairs,' Katherine suggested when she couldn't find anything else to wash or dry.

It was a good job they'd eaten well at their impromptu reception because the nervous butterflies fluttering around in her stomach had made it almost impossible to eat now.

She wondered if that was why Damon had seemed so quiet.

Where once they would have chatted non-stop over a meal, their conversation tonight had been limited to little more than monosyllables on either side.

Silently, she followed Damon out into the hallway and retrieved her small suitcase. Her mother had been aghast that she was taking so little, and Katherine had been unable to tell her that she'd hardly been packing for a typical honeymoon.

If she'd had any idea that she was going to change her mind about the permanence of their arrangement, she would certainly have thought twice about packing her comfortable but strictly unglamorous nightshirts. They certainly wouldn't help her in her plan to change Damon's mind.

She followed him up the stairs and was surprised to see a small posy of silk flowers attached to the door of the master bedroom.

'What on earth...?' she muttered, and put her case down to explore.

She swung the door wide as she switched the light on and gasped when she saw the efforts that had gone into making the room a honeymooners' dream come true.

'Your mother said she'd left everything ready but obviously she didn't know that this wasn't going to be the usual sort of honeymoon,' Damon said gruffly. 'I presume there's another room that I can use?'

It took Katherine several seconds to compose herself after Damon's calm dismissal. He hadn't even commented on the beautiful flowers let alone the way the enormous double bed was turned down so invitingly. Was he totally unaffected by the symbolism?

'My old room is just along here,' she said tautly, leading the way along the corridor. 'That's my grand-mother's and the next one is mother's,' she said as they passed the next two doors. 'This is the guest room and the last one is mine.'

She twisted the handle and flung the door open, reaching out automatically to flick the light on.

'Oh, my God!' she breathed in horror at the sight that met her eyes. 'What on earth have they been doing?'

It certainly wasn't *her* room any more, that was certain. Every stick of furniture had been removed, the floor covered with dropcloths and assorted ladders and pasting tables that had been used when the walls had been stripped and repapered. In one corner was a pile of boxes full of nursery furniture just waiting to be assembled.

'It's a nursery!' she exclaimed in a mixture of delight and dismay when she took in the pretty border of rabbits and baby deer. 'What on earth possessed them to…?'

She ground to an embarrassed halt when the obvious answer came to her.

'It's for *our* baby,' she whispered in a choked voice, hardly able to see Damon's face for the emotional tears flooding her eyes.

'I'd say this was pretty good evidence that we've

managed to convince them with our bogus marriage,' he agreed calmly. He was leaning against the frame of the door as though unwilling to even set foot inside the room.

'Clearly it's more than a little premature in view of the fact we've only been married for about eight hours,' he continued. 'I presume the guest room will be available?'

Katherine could have hit him.

How could he be so calm and unemotional about this beautiful room? Hadn't it immediately made him imagine the child who would gaze out of his cot at these enchanting animals? Their child?

Obviously not, if the closed expression on his face was anything to go by.

'If the bed isn't made up it won't take long for me to do it,' she said coldly as she marched back along the corridor to the next room. 'I'm sure you'll be very—'

Her eyes and mouth dropped open at the sight that met her eyes. This room was in an even worse state because every spare inch of space was stuffed with the furniture from her room.

The silence stretched out between them until it became decidedly uncomfortable, then Damon cleared his throat.

'If you would like to find the spare bedding, I presume there's a couch or settee somewhere that I can use?'

He turned and walked away from her, only stopping when he reached the suitcase he'd deposited outside the door of the master bedroom.

Katherine's eyes tracked him helplessly every inch of the way, admiring the way his broad shoulders and narrow waist were complemented by the cut of his suit. She was still watching him when he turned to look back at her over his shoulder and she felt almost guilty for being caught.

'If that's what you want,' she muttered under her breath then pasted a sweet smile on her face as she made for the linen cupboard.

The smile grew more genuine when she suddenly realised that Damon would have no option but to share a room with her when they moved into his flat. There was only the one room and one bed.

He might have managed to put a serious crimp in her plans, but it was only a temporary one. In two days' time she would begin her campaign in earnest.

She knew he was attracted to her, she'd had the visible proof that she could arouse him. Now she needed to use that basic attraction to work on his emotions.

Courting Dr Cade—*that's* what she'd call her crusade, and he wasn't going to stand a chance against her because from now on she was going to be pulling out all the stops.

Katherine was lying on the bed, staring up at the subtle shadows cast on the ceiling by the pretty bedside lamps.

It had probably been her grandmother's idea to revamp the room, but she could easily detect the signs of her mother's input in the quietly elegant style.

It was a shame that they had gone to all that effort, but she was glad they would never have to know that it hadn't been appreciated.

Still, enough about the room. Now was the time for some serious planning.

She'd suggested that Damon use the bathroom first

to give her a little more time to think. Soon it would be time to approach him with that age-old ploy.

Katherine heard the sound of the lock on the bathroom door and sprang to her feet.

'Stage one,' she whispered as she hurried across the room on stockinged feet and swung her door silently open.

He was still wearing his suit trousers but was beautifully naked from the waist up, the soft lighting in the hallway making his skin look almost as if it had been cast in bronze.

'Ah, Damon,' she called as he was just about to start on his way down the stairs to his makeshift bed in the sitting room.

He whirled to face her as if she'd just shot at him.

'If you've got a minute… I'm afraid I can't get out of my dress without a bit of help.'

She turned her back to him to demonstrate her problem. When her mother had fastened the row of silk-covered buttons that marched the length of her back she'd never dreamt that she might have to use them as a means of drawing Damon closer to her.

There hadn't been very many of them, but the few kisses they'd shared had been so instantaneously explosive that they certainly hadn't led her to believe that there would be any problem with intimacy between them.

She didn't know whether he'd done it deliberately, but she distinctly heard Damon sigh heavily before he deposited his wash kit at the top of the stairs and made his way towards her along the corridor.

Sheer nerves tempted her to chatter about the difficulties of undoing so many buttons without help but she bit her tongue.

Silently, she turned her back towards him and slid her fingers through her hair to lift it out of his way.

Equally silently he began to slip each button out of its accompanying rouleau loop.

For an awful moment she thought he was totally unaffected by what he was doing, even though he must surely be able to see the sexy underwear she'd hidden underneath the dress.

Then her calm, steady-as-a-rock doctor fumbled, not once but twice.

She had to force herself to stifle a sigh of relief but she couldn't curb the wicked smile that crept over her face.

She waited until he'd nearly reached the end of the row before she spoke.

'Oh, by the way, you remember you said we wouldn't have any problem with our luggage because it had been locked securely in your car?'

He grunted so she took the sound as agreement and carried on. 'Well, you must have reckoned without having traitors in the camp. I hardly recognise a single thing in my case. Just look at this nightie my mother put in.'

She reached for the scrap of silk and lace draped conveniently nearby and held it up by the spaghetti straps.

'It's gorgeous, isn't it?' she commented, revelling in the stunned expression frozen on his face. 'Not the sort of thing I usually choose for myself but I'm going to thoroughly enjoy wearing it. Silk feels so...*sensuous* against naked skin, doesn't it?'

She leaned forward to drape it across the foot of the bed and, as if by accident, allowed the dress to slip forward off her shoulders.

'Oops!' She grabbed for it and held it coyly against her, all the while knowing that he'd already seen what she wanted him to see—the equally decadent bra her mother had given her just this morning. Until she'd put it on she hadn't appreciated just how clever bra design had become. She'd certainly never expected to look as if she filled anything more than a thirty-four B, let alone a thirty-six D.

Now that she was facing him she had to try to hide her smile but it was very hard, especially when she realised that Damon didn't only become aroused when she watched him get undressed. It obviously happened just as easily when he watched *her* getting undressed, too.

'If that's all you needed,' he said, sounding slightly strangled as he turned away.

He left the room too quickly to hear her reply.

'No. It's not all I needed,' she murmured softly. 'But it'll do for now.'

A broad grin painted her face as she licked the tip of one finger and wrote an imaginary figure in the air.

'Score one,' she added with a little chuckle.

It wasn't as good as looking forward to sharing her bed with him tonight, but it was a start.

It was probably because of the emotional overload that she'd dozed off so quickly, but she couldn't have been asleep for long when she was jerked to wakefulness by the sound of the front doorbell.

'Who on earth is that?' she mumbled as she flipped the covers back and hurried across to the window.

One glance was enough to stop her heart. She knew that car too well to mistake it.

'Damon,' she called breathlessly, having run all the way down the stairs. 'Damon, wake up.'

She hesitated for just one split second, her hand hovering above his naked shoulder before she grabbed it and shook.

'What is it?' he said, apparently firing on all cylinders as soon as his eyes were open. Was that what medical training did for you?

'Kat? What are you doing here?' he demanded and shook his head, obviously not as lucid as she'd thought. When he sat up in the bed the covers fell in a precarious heap on his lap but there wasn't time to wonder exactly how much he was, or wasn't, wearing.

'They're here,' she said hoarsely, glancing fearfully over her shoulder in the direction of the front door.

'Who's here?'

'My mother and my grandmother,' she said just as the bell rang again. How he hadn't heard it the first time she didn't know. 'They're at the door now.'

It took about two seconds before he realised the significance of what she was saying. She could almost hear the penny drop.

There was no way they could persuade her family that they'd married for love if he was spending the first night of their honeymoon on the settee in the sitting room.

CHAPTER SEVEN

'DAMMIT,' Damon swore as he flung the covers aside and reached for his trousers. Katherine didn't even have a chance to notice what he was wearing.

'Grab the bedclothes and the rest of my stuff and take it upstairs,' he directed, automatically taking charge of the situation as he would do at the hospital. 'I'll give you long enough to get out of sight, then I'll open the door for them.'

Without turning on a light, it was difficult to be certain that she'd found everything, but there wasn't time to check.

Her heart was hammering in her chest as she tried to hurry up the stairs with the corners of sheets and blankets tangling around her legs. She didn't know how she managed it but she heard Damon sliding the chain off the door just as she flung herself into the bedroom and out of sight.

She could barely hear what was happening in the hallway over the sound of her laboured breathing, but was conscious that it was imperative she appear down there as soon as possible.

Tempted to dump her burden where she stood, she turned the light on and forced herself to separate out the bedding then stuff it into the bottom of the empty wardrobe.

The sight of movement out of the corner of her eye had her confronting her image in a full-length mirror and she realised for the first time exactly how enticing her nightdress was.

It was one thing to wave it in front of Damon to whet his appetite but it was another thing entirely to confront him in it in front of her family.

'Of course, she unpacked my nice thick chenille dressing-gown,' she moaned, desperate not to have to waste time getting dressed before she went down. Heaven only knew what they were talking about down there.

With a flash of inspiration she grabbed Damon's crumpled shirt, barely pausing to force her arms into the sleeves as she hurried towards the stairs.

'What's happened?' she demanded as she joined the rest of them, her arms wrapped around her to hold the front of the shirt closed. It was nearly the same length as her nightdress but she still felt as if she were parading in front of Damon half-naked.

Where had all this evening's bravado gone?

'We're so sorry, darling,' her mother said looking quite crestfallen as she fiddled with the car keys. 'We really can't understand how it happened, but when we got to the hotel we found there had been some sort of mix up with the reservations—there were no rooms booked for us.'

'Well, what else could we do but come home?' her grandmother added.

Katherine glanced from one to the other then looked at Damon. She had a definite feeling that there was something strange going on here and she wouldn't be at all surprised if Damon agreed with her.

'Well, I'm just sorry we took so long to open the door to you,' he said quietly. 'You must have been worried that we weren't going to wake up. You might have ended up sleeping in the car for the night.'

There was a strange silence following his words and when she caught the sideways glance between the two older women she was almost certain that their late arrival was part of some scheme.

Had they guessed that there was something fishy going on between Damon and herself? What had they done to give themselves away? Had this late night arrival been intended to catch them out?

'It doesn't make any sense,' she protested when they'd all finally trooped their way upstairs. 'If they had any suspicions about our reasons for getting married, surely they would have said something *before* it took place.'

'Instead of that, they almost seemed to be pushing us on,' Damon said thoughtfully. 'I thought it was just because they were pleased you were finally getting married, and especially because you were doing it in time to save them from having to move.'

'That's why I can't understand tonight's little scene,' Katherine continued. 'It just doesn't make sense if they were trying to prove that we'd faked the whole thing. Anyway, they couldn't know that because they don't know that I overheard them talking about Grandfather's will.'

'And we can't confront them about it until we're certain that the solicitor has accepted that the conditions of the will have been complied with,' Damon concluded grimly.

'So we're stuck with it, either way,' she said slowly, the true consequences of her words only coming home to her as she heard the words spoken aloud.

She didn't honestly know how she felt about the situation.

It had been one thing to plan to court Damon Cade into admitting he loved her; it was another thing entirely to have him feel as if her family was pressuring him into staying with her against his will.

Her little ploy with the buttons on her dress and waving her nightdress in front of him just seemed tawdry now.

She had been feeling excited about the prospect of trying out her fledgling seduction techniques. Now, all she wanted to do was climb under the covers and pull them right up over her head.

'Enough, Kat,' Damon said, breaking into her spiralling thoughts. 'You've been under tension for over two weeks and after the events of today…' He shook his head. 'What you need is to switch off your brain and get some sleep. Perhaps it will all look different in the morning.'

'You wish!' she exclaimed, for the first time feeling the burn of tears welling up. 'So far, every day seems to get worse. I'm almost afraid to shut my eyes.'

'Kat, would a cuddle from a friend help?' he offered softly.

For a moment she wasn't certain whether she'd heard him correctly, but one glance at his open arms had her hurrying willingly into their shelter.

'Oh, Damon, I'm so sorry I got you involved in all this,' she wailed, trying to bury herself against his warmth and his strength. 'I'm surprised you still want to be my friend.'

'Shh…' he soothed. 'Don't cry, little Kat. You'll have your family breaking in here, wanting to know what I'm doing to you, and I absolutely refuse to do anything with an audience.'

Katherine gave a hiccup of laughter at his nonsense and the threat of tears was banished for a while.

'Oh, Damon, I'm so tired,' she admitted. 'Tired of trying to keep secrets, tired of pretending and just plain tired.'

'Come on, then, let's get you into bed.' He turned her towards the acres of rumpled bedding, one arm still wrapped comfortingly around her shoulders as he flipped the covers aside. 'Do you want to take my shirt off before you lie down?'

She glanced down at herself and shook her head.

'Not with the lights on,' she declared with feeling. 'The silkworms who made this thing must have been on half-rations—there's nothing to it!'

Damon muttered under his breath something that sounded like, 'That's why I like it.' But she didn't bother to ask him to repeat it. She'd had enough of trying to be provocative for one day.

He waited until she'd made herself comfortable then pulled the covers right up to her chin.

'Sleep well,' he murmured, reaching out to turn off her bedside light, then straightening up to his full height.

'You're not going away?' she demanded, raising herself up onto one elbow to grab his hand. 'Please, Damon, don't leave me. Anyway, there isn't anywhere else for you to sleep.'

'I was going to unearth the bedding you brought up and set it out on the floor. I presume you hid it somewhere in here?'

'Yes, in the wardrobe. But you can't use it,' she insisted. 'If they've gone to this much trouble to keep us company on this excuse for a honeymoon, my grandmother will probably insist on bringing us breakfast in bed.'

'If she insists on bringing us breakfast in bed on our honeymoon then I hope she's prepared for the consequences,' he growled darkly as he strode round to the other side of the bed.

'Consequences?' she repeated uneasily, sliding a little further under the covers as she watched him release the catch on the waistband of his trousers.

She'd pulled the covers up just high enough to mask what he was doing by the time she heard the muted sound of his zip, but his chuckle was all too clear.

'Coward,' she heard him whisper as she felt the mattress sink down on his side of the bed.

'Windermere Ward. Sister Gillard—uh, sorry, Sister Cade speaking,' Katherine announced when she grabbed the phone. After only two days she wasn't accustomed to using her new name yet.

'Hello, Sister Cade, Dr Cade here,' Damon said with a chuckle in his voice. 'I'm bringing up a young lady to join you. Sally Cronin. She's fourteen, badly malnourished and suffering from smoke inhalation and burns.'

'How bad are the burns?' she asked, trying very hard to ignore her reaction to the sound of his voice.

'Mainly superficial but a couple will need watching. We've got her on oxygen to help her lungs. See you in a few minutes.'

Her heart turned another somersault in spite of her attempt at calm. 'For heaven's sake,' she muttered under her breath, 'you live with the man now. You've even been sleeping in the same bed. It's hardly earth-shattering that you'll be seeing him in a couple of minutes.'

But it didn't matter how often she lectured herself. The initial attraction two years ago had grown out of all recognition, especially now that she was living so closely with him.

Perhaps that was the problem, she thought as she quickly checked that the bed was ready for Sally's arrival. The two of them were now sharing Damon's flat, and their meals, but absolutely nothing of a more intimate nature. If their relationship had become a sexual one maybe she wouldn't be quite so obsessed with him.

She pulled a face when she thought about their strange honeymoon, wondering how many other newly-wed husbands would have spent those two precious days with their in-laws and their nights on the opposite side of the bed.

'Here we are, then, love,' announced the porter as he swung the ward doors open and clipped them back so that he could bring the trolley through. 'There's Sister all ready and waiting for you. You'll be all right.'

He and his partner swung their burden expertly into position and with the minimum of fuss she was transferred to the ward bed.

Katherine was glad she'd had plenty of practice at keeping a straight face. That was the only thing that stopped her reacting when she saw exactly how thin the youngster was.

'Hello, Sally. I'm Sister Cade,' she said, still with a slight hesitation before she gave her name.

'You're getting better,' Damon murmured in her ear, and she jumped. She'd been so busy concentrating on her latest charge that she hadn't noticed him arrive.

The youngster looked from one to the other with red-rimmed eyes then lifted a blistered paw totally enclosed in a plastic bag to raise the oxygen mask a little.

'Same name,' she croaked with a brief show of interest.

'That's because we're married,' Damon agreed equally briefly. 'Now, promise you'll tell Sister if the pain relief we've given you isn't enough.'

Sally looked away from him dismissively. 'Yeah, yeah,' she murmured, and made a great pretence of examining her surroundings.

'Is someone going to be bringing your things in for you?' Katherine asked, realising that the usual bundle of belongings was completely absent.

'No,' she said baldly.

'Well, do you want me to ring someone for you? Patients usually like to have a few of their own things around when they're in—'

'I said no,' the youngster snapped, suddenly almost shaking with something that looked strangely like fury when she had to force the words out through a smoke-damaged throat.

'That means no to _everything_,' she continued, her voice growing more and more hoarse. 'Nobody will be bringing in any personal belongings for me because I haven't got any personal belongings.' She held up her hands. 'Everything got burnt.'

'Everything?' Katherine repeated in horror, trying to imagine what it would be like to be left without a possession to her name.

'Everything, including my gran,' Sally said, and burst into tears.

Katherine met Damon's eyes and sent him silent questions about the exact circumstances of Sally's injuries. He nodded and as he strode swiftly away she knew that he would be initiating enquiries about Sally's grandmother.

Katherine shuddered at the very idea of her own precious grandmother being caught in a fire, but it was Sally's situation that demanded her concentration now.

'You were both in the house when the fire started?' she questioned gently, handing Sally a handful of paper hankies.

It was several minutes and a coughing fit before Sally replied.

'She caused the fire,' she said in a tiny voice, her little face suddenly grey with exhaustion and very strange-looking without eyebrows and with the front of her hair burnt away. It made her look so naked and vulnerable somehow.

'She likes to have a smoke but when it's too cold to get up she smokes in bed. She must have fallen asleep and…' The tears began again.

Katherine swiftly settled one hip on the edge of the bed and wrapped a comforting arm around Sally's bony shoulders.

'Hey, sweetheart, I'm sorry,' she murmured, gently stroking her hand up and down the oversized gown covering the skinny arm. She was careful to keep the pressure light enough not to aggravate any of the youngster's injuries.

Crying seemed to set Sally coughing and Katherine was sorry that she was forced to stop before she'd been able to cry all the pain out.

'Can you tell me a bit about your gran?' she prompted, willing to match the girl story for story with tales about her own grandmother if it would help her to remember the good times. 'How long have you been staying with her?'

'My mother dumped me on her when I started walk-ing,' Sally said baldly. 'Gran said Mum didn't want me any more when I learned how to climb out of my cot 'cos that meant I could come into her room when she had a man with her.'

Katherine swallowed, desperately trying to find something to say. Nothing materialised in the space that used to be her brain. On a ward filled with teen-agers from every level of society she'd learned to ig-nore all sorts of language and bad manners, but Sally's matter-of-fact acceptance of the degradation of her childhood innocence shocked her.

'It was all right with Gran...mostly,' she continued, almost in a monotone. 'Except she likes to drink gin more than she likes to eat, so there was no food in the house. Still, Social Security made sure her rent was paid so we had somewhere to live.'

Katherine knew from the way she pressed her lips tightly together that Sally had suddenly remembered that she no longer had somewhere to live. Her heart ached for the young girl, wondering what on earth would happen to her now.

'Will I have scars?' Sally demanded softly, the words almost lost in the hiss of the oxygen.

Katherine had a feeling that the child could only stand so much honesty at this point so chose to hedge.

'I haven't seen all of your injuries yet, apart from your hands and a couple of blisters on your arms and your face. Dr Cade told me that most of your injuries were superficial, which means that they would nor-mally be healed within seven to ten days.' On a nor-mally healthy child, she added to herself.

'Some areas of skin will stay pink for several days,

weeks or even months after that, but that tends to gradually fade away without you even noticing it's gone.'

'And the rest?' Her direct gaze went from Katherine
to her hands and back again and she wouldn't let
Katherine off the hook.

'That will depend on things such as your diet—'

'*I* don't need to diet!' the girl exclaimed on a choked
laugh, holding an arm out towards Katherine. 'You'd
need three of me to make one of these supermodels.'

'I didn't mean diet like that,' Katherine explained.
'I meant taking in extra protein and vitamins and min-
erals so your body can repair itself properly and fight
off any infections.'

Sally subsided with a nod of comprehension and
Katherine made a mental note to be present when her
dressings were changed. It might be that direct appli-
cation of vitamin E would help to prevent scarring on
some of the worst areas. She'd have to speak to Damon
about that.

As if thinking about him had conjured him out of
thin air, she caught sight of him striding across the
ward towards them.

'Sally, I've just been speaking to the police and the
paramedics,' he said as he sat himself on the opposite
side of the bed. 'They told me to give you a couple of
messages, and the most important one is that your gran
is still alive. You managed to get her out before the
smoke from the fire could kill her.'

'What?' Her face was a picture of disbelief. 'She's
still alive? But she *can't* be. She wasn't even breathing
and she was all grey and…and floppy.'

'Well, I promise you I'm telling you the truth. In
fact, when her doctor gives us the OK that she's ready
for visitors, I'll make sure you're taken up to see her.'

Sally looked up at him out of suddenly brimming eyes, obviously speechless at the news.

'And that leaves me with the second message,' he continued with a smile. 'The police and ambulancemen told me to tell you that after what you did today they're putting your name in for a bravery award. If you hadn't kept your head and remembered all the right things to do, neither you nor your gran would be alive now.'

'Poor kid,' Katherine murmured as Damon drove them to his flat.

Today their shifts had coincided but tomorrow she was going to have to walk to the hospital because she wouldn't start till later.

'Which kid?' Damon asked with a chuckle in his voice. 'You've got a whole ward full of them.'

'Sally.' She shook her head. 'Every time I've looked at her today I couldn't help wondering how I would have felt if I'd been the one lying there, believing that my last relative had just died.'

'By all accounts, her gran isn't exactly the best person to have charge of children. She's barely able to take care of herself.'

'But she's still a blood relative,' Katherine insisted. 'That must be important, to know that there's at least one other person…'

It took the deliberately blank expression on Damon's face before she realised what her rambling words must be doing to him.

'Oh, Damon, I'm so sorry,' she whispered, horrified at the pain she must have caused him by bringing up the topic. 'For a moment I'd completely forgotten—'

'It's all right, Kat. Nothing to worry about,' he interrupted flatly. 'It's all in the past now, anyway.'

But it wasn't.

She knew from the expressionless way he spoke that the wrenching pain of losing one member of his family after another would never be relegated to the status of an unimportant series of distant events.

For heaven's sake, those tragic losses were the reason why he'd sworn never to marry, never to allow himself to become close to anyone for fear that he would lose them, too.

'Damon,' she began, hoping she could find the words that would allow her behind the screen he erected between himself and the rest of the world.

'Do we need to do any shopping?' he broke in, deliberately changing the topic of conversation. 'I can't remember how much we've got in the line of fresh fruit and vegetables.'

Katherine dearly wanted to clear the air between them as quickly as possible but was sensitive enough to realise that now was not a good time.

'There are several things we need to stock up on,' she admitted, resigned to the chore of visiting the local supermarket. There would certainly be no chance for heart-to-heart discussions there.

She tried to imagine it—a bag of onions in one hand and carrots in the other while she gazed into his eyes and asked, 'Why don't you fancy me, Damon?'

She subdued a snort of self-mockery then nearly laughed aloud when she noticed the funny looks the elderly gentleman was giving her while he gave her a wide berth.

Later would obviously have to do, even if she had to wait until they were lying in bed together… It wasn't as if they did anything else while they were lying there, she thought sadly.

And she'd had such high hopes.

Once she'd realised how much she loved him she'd presumed that things would more or less spontaneously happen the way nature intended—after all, wasn't marriage supposed to combine the maximum of temptation with the maximum of opportunity?

So far, not only had the opportunities been limited, firstly by Damon's disappointing insistence on sleeping in the sitting room and then by her family's presence, but it also seemed as though, despite previous evidence to the contrary, Damon wasn't even tempted by her.

Reminding him of the reasons he'd never wanted to marry in the first place, that hadn't been very helpful either. She would have to clear the air between them if she was ever going to succeed at her ultimate goal.

It wasn't as if he didn't like her, she thought as he insisted on pushing the laden trolley. He even tossed her a wicked grin when she caught him slipping an extra packet of chocolate biscuits under some cleaning materials.

She felt a familiar shiver run through her when she saw that smile. The first time it had happened was when she'd been introduced to him as the new member of staff.

It had taken her all of thirty seconds to realise that if he'd felt the same attraction he was far too intensely focused on his career to do anything about it. Their discussion just a few days later had only confirmed his unavailability by giving her an insight into the causes of his withdrawal into himself.

For two years she'd had to be content with working beside him, grateful for the friendship that meant she'd been the one he'd invited to accompany him to staff functions.

Sometimes she'd berated herself for settling for so little. Surely there must have been many other men who would have been willing to offer her their hearts and hands. The trouble had been that she hadn't been able to find anyone else who'd interested her when the only one with whom she'd been able to envision sharing her life was Damon Cade.

Now she was married to the man—had been for all of three days—and she was no closer to him than she had been before the ceremony.

In fact, he seemed even *less* relaxed around her now than he had before.

He even offered to unpack and put away all the shopping when the two of them kept colliding in his tiny kitchen.

'It would be better if I stayed to help,' she pointed out, perversely taking heart from the fact that he was apparently disturbed by the way they couldn't help touching. 'I need to know where you keep things if I'm going to be able to find them again.'

'Oh, but you don't need—'

'Had you had any thoughts about what you'd like to eat tonight?' she forged on, determined he wasn't going to rob her of any chance to be a real part of his life. 'I'd thought it would be quick and easy to do a stir-fry with lots of vegetables. How good are you at chopping?'

He was stiff at first, as though he felt he'd been forced into doing something he didn't want to, but when the onions made her cry and she didn't have a hand free to grab a square of kitchen towel to mop up, he did it for her.

The trouble was, his proximity while he'd persuaded her to blow her nose like a little girl had made his eyes water too, and they'd both ended up giggling like a couple of kids.

'Oh, this is so good!' he exclaimed with the first mouthful still in his mouth, a blissful expression on his face. 'And it was so simple.'

'Everything's simple once you know how,' she said with a shrug, secretly relishing his pleasure. They said that the way to a man's heart was through his stomach, so perhaps if she were to cook for him she could persuade him to fall in love with her.

He even insisted on helping with the clearing away after the meal. Then she suggested taking a cup of coffee through to the sitting room and investigating the programmes available on the television and it was as if a switch had flicked off inside his head.

In the blink of an eye the friendly, teasing man she'd just spent a couple of hours with was gone.

'I'm sorry, but I've got some work to do before I can go to bed,' he said quickly.

'But—'

'Don't let it stop you,' he offered with a gesture towards the large screen sitting blankly in the corner. 'If there's something you want to watch.'

There was nothing she wanted to watch, she thought crossly as she watched him disappear into his tiny study. The whole point had been for the two of them to spend time together so that they could start to build up the sort of relationship that could last a lifetime.

Still, if he had work to do, then he had work to do, she conceded glumly as she flicked through the channels. Now she would have to fill the evening with the same old boring things she used to do before they were married.

It was a self-improvement programme that gave her

an alternative idea. Why not spend a couple of hours pampering herself with a bath and a manicure and whatever else came to mind so that when Damon came to bed she would be totally irresistible?

After she'd filled the bath with sweetly scented bubbles and sunk in them up to her neck she suddenly realised that she was having fun.

This was the first time she'd ever deliberately treated herself to a leisurely bath in the knowledge that she would be sharing her bed with a man afterwards.

It hadn't been the same at her grandmother's house. That first night Damon had made certain she'd understood that he would be sleeping downstairs, and after that it just hadn't felt right to plan a seduction when her family had been there too.

This time she was going to make full use of all those beauty aids her friends and colleagues had been giving her each birthday and Christmas.

An hour and a half later she left the bathroom full of pretty smells, shaved, exfoliated, buffed and moisturised to within an inch of her life.

Her hair was so clean and shiny that it had squeaked when she was rinsing it. Now it gleamed as she ran her brush through the long strands and left them to lie over her shoulders like a dark honey waterfall.

'Nails next,' she muttered to herself. Not that much needed doing to them. They had to be kept short and neat for the sake of her job and if she put nail varnish on them now she would only have to take it off again in the morning. She could hardly go into work tomorrow with them painted blood red.

'But that doesn't mean I can't have scarlet toenails,' she said with a gleeful smile as she lithely folded herself into a pretzel and began to paint.

The smile had dimmed somewhat by the time midnight arrived.

She'd finished all her preparations and had donned the beautiful nightdress her mother had sneakily given her for the first night of the honeymoon, then had taken herself to their bed with a romantic novel to while away the time until Damon had finished his work.

She knew that the responsibilities of Damon's job involved many hours of paperwork, on top of the time he spent with the patients, but when the hands met at the top of the clock she decided that enough was enough.

She slid out of the lovely warm bed and paused for a moment in thought. After all her efforts this evening, her old chenille dressing-gown was hardly in keeping with the seductive image she was trying to get Damon to notice.

Unfortunately, she didn't think she had quite enough courage to go looking for him dressed in just her skimpy nightie. It was certainly far more revealing than anything else she'd ever owned, and the idea of brazenly walking into Damon's study with most of her…assets clearly visible was enough to have her reaching for Damon's thick towelling robe.

She padded silently along the short hallway, not bothering to turn on the light as she aimed straight for the thin band of yellow escaping around the edge of the study door.

'Damon?' she called as she gave a little tap, then she tried to push the door of his study open, intending just to stick her head round the edge to speak to him. She could just have a quick word with him and be back in bed by the time he arrived so that he could still get the full seductive effect.

Except that she couldn't open the door. It only moved a couple of inches before it came to a complete halt against something heavy.

Suddenly Katherine had visions of Damon lying unconscious on the floor, his body wedged against the door so that she would be unable to get into the room to help him.

'Damon!' she called again and rapped her knuckles sharply on the door. 'Damon, can you hear me? Are you all right?'

CHAPTER EIGHT

THERE was a sudden groaning sound on the other side of the door and Katherine froze, waiting for the noise to come again.

It did, accompanied by a strange slithering.

'Damon! Are you all right?' She leaned against the door, pressing her ear against the wood as she tried to decipher what was happening in there.

There was another noise and she leaned even harder, but suddenly whatever had been against the door was no longer there.

The door flew open before she could straighten up and she was so badly unbalanced that she immediately began to fall.

'Kat! What on earth are you doing?' Damon demanded, only just managing to grab her arm to prevent her falling flat on her face. 'I thought you went to bed hours ago.'

Katherine was so glad to see that he wasn't lying on the floor dead or dying that she didn't know whether to hug him or strangle him.

'What do you mean, what am I doing?' she retorted. 'What were *you* doing?' She shrugged off his restraining hand and whirled to pace out into the hallway and back again. There was too much adrenaline racing through her for her to stand still.

'I tried to open the door to talk to you and there was something heavy in the way. Then you groaned and I called you again but you didn't answer. I thought you'd collapsed and needed medical attention, for heaven's sake!' she finished, flinging her hands up in the air.

Katherine was well aware that the gesture would have been more impressive if her hands hadn't been completely buried in the sleeves of his robe. As it was, she had a feeling that she looked far more like the smallest of the seven dwarves, and it didn't help her temper to cool.

'I wasn't groaning,' he denied, rubbing one hand over his rumpled hair in an exasperated gesture of his own. 'I was busy.'

'Busy behind the door, making groaning noises?' she demanded sceptically. 'Is this some perversion they haven't covered in the late-night chat shows?'

'Oh, for heaven's sake!' he exclaimed, and took a single stride forward to grab her arm.

It didn't occur to her for a moment to be afraid of him, even when he began to pull her into his study. She had never seen him anything less than gentle and controlled with any of his patients, no matter how stroppy, and knew violence was outside his nature.

'Come here and look, woman,' he growled. 'When you were knocking on the door I'd just picked that box up off the top of a pile behind the door. I wasn't exactly in the position to hold a conversation with you because I've made the mistake of filling the damn thing with books and made it too heavy.

'As to why they were behind the door,' he continued, not allowing her time to utter a word to save her embarrassment, 'you will note, please, that *that* is the only empty space left in the room.'

It only took a cursory glance around the cramped space to see that he was right. There was only a square

yard of floor left empty now, that same square yard
that the two of them were now occupying.

'I thought you were working,' she said, puzzled that
his overcrowded but relatively well-organised room
was now a shambles.

Then it dawned on her what he'd been doing.

'Oh, Damon, you've started sorting through your
brother's things,' she said softly, understanding completely why his mood might be brittle. 'Why didn't you
tell me? I could have helped.'

To her disappointment he released her hand and
turned away from her, shaking his head.

'No, Kat. This is something I need to do for myself,'
he said in a husky voice. 'There are a few ghosts I
need to confront and it's probably easier if I face them
by myself.'

'OK,' she whispered softly, accepting that he knew
best how he could cope with the overload of memories
he was going to unearth. 'But, promise me, if you find
you want to talk about anything—whether it's reminis-
cences about your childhood or exasperation because
there really are alien life forms in the bottom of the
boxes—you'll come and tell me about it.'

While she was speaking he'd turned to face her again
and he was silent for several seconds, his eyes very
intent on her face, almost as though he wanted to be
able to read her mind.

Finally, one side of his mouth lifted in a slight grin
and he gave a single nod.

'OK,' he said. 'I promise I'll come to you if I need
to talk.'

He didn't sound as if he thought that was very likely,
but she was pleased with the concession.

'Now, how about knocking off?' she demanded

lightly. 'You've been working in here for hours and it's gone midnight. Time you were in bed.'

She saw his eyes flicker over her, apparently only just taking in the fact that she'd borrowed his dressing-gown again. What *she* hadn't noticed until that moment was that the belt wasn't tied as tightly as she would have liked.

Perhaps it had become loosened when he'd rescued her from her near fall or when she'd been marching backwards and forwards, waving her arms around. Whatever the cause, she'd only just discovered that the lacy top of her honeymoon nightdress was now displayed in all its revealing glory between the lapels of the robe.

Suddenly Damon whirled away from her and reached for a haphazard pile of journals.

'You go and tuck yourself under the covers again,' he suggested. 'I'll just shift a couple of things so I can still get to my desk to do paperwork, and then I'll go to the bathroom.'

It was almost as if he'd been avoiding looking at her, she mused from the warmth of the bedclothes a couple of minutes later. Was it because of the amount of pale flesh on view through the lacy fabric?

As soon as she'd noticed how much she was revealing, Katherine had automatically wrapped the dressing-gown more firmly around herself.

Perhaps covering up had been a mistake, she pondered as she waited for her toes to warm up. If she'd stood there with all her charms on show, perhaps he'd have been a little more eager to join her in bed. He didn't even seem to have noticed her flaming red toenails.

*   *   *

An annoying beeping was trying to drag her out of a wonderful dream.

Katherine tried to close her ears to it but she was being inexorably drawn towards wakefulness.

She wanted to wallow just a little longer in the fantasy that Damon was beside her in bed with his arms wrapped around her and his lips pressing warm kisses to the back of her neck. It was a favourite dream of hers, one she'd been secretly indulging in for two years now, and it just seemed to have become more vivid as time had gone on.

The last two nights, staying at her grandmother's house, had been a refined sort of torture. To have shared a bed with him, knowing that he wasn't even going to come close enough to touch her, had brought frustration to a new level. Then there had been the disappointment of waking up each morning to find that he was already up and gone.

Perhaps his tantalising proximity was why her dreams had suddenly grown more realistic.

Take this morning's version, for instance. She could almost swear that she could feel the soft warmth of his breath stirring strands of her hair against her cheek. And his heart. She was certain she could feel the way it was beating against her back.

It was almost as though her favourite dream had actually become real, as if she could turn over and find herself face to face with...

'Damon!' she gasped as she suddenly realised that he really *was* still in the bed with her. And not only that—he wasn't lying right on the other edge.

Because she'd turned over they were lying almost face to face, his sleepy blue eyes navy against the plain white pillow.

'Good morning, Kat,' he murmured, the hand lying across her waist moving almost reflexively, as if he couldn't help savouring the sensation of the silky fabric of her nightie against his fingers.

Suddenly he seemed to realise what he was doing and began to roll away. 'If you'll excuse me…?'

'Wait! Where are you going?' She grabbed hold of his hand before he could withdraw from the contact completely. This was the closest they'd ever been—if you didn't count the time she'd landed on top of him— and she wasn't nearly ready for it to end.

'I'm going to turn that alarm off before it drives me mad,' he said, and smacked one hand on top of it. 'Ah! Peace!' he exclaimed and flopped back down onto the pillow, his arms folded across the naked width of his chest.

Katherine couldn't help staring at him. It seemed so intimate to be close enough to see the creases left on his face by the pillow, and each individual hair that made up the dark shadow of his emerging beard.

She had no idea whether he'd shaved before he came to bed last night because she'd— 'Oh, Damon, I'm so sorry,' she exclaimed when she realised where her thoughts had taken her. 'I fell asleep before you came to bed.'

'That's all right. You probably needed the sleep,' he said easily, barely flicking her a glance.

'No, it's not all right,' she contradicted, nettled by the fact that he didn't even seem to care. 'I spent an hour and a half last night pampering myself with a bubble bath and a hair-wash and a manicure, ready for you to come to bed, and then I fell asleep before you got here.'

Katherine suddenly realised what her pique had led

her into confessing and suddenly wished that this conversation *was* part of her dream.

She groaned and pulled the covers up over her flaming face. How *could* she have told him something as embarrassing as that?

It was one thing to make up her mind to seduce the man, but to come right out and tell him about all her preparations...and then to fall asleep before she could put them to use... She groaned again.

'Kat?' She felt him take hold of the edge of the covers and try to lift them but she tightened her grip.

'Go away, *please*,' she demanded, mortified.

If only she weren't so inexperienced she would have known how to go about such things. She should have practised her wiles on a few more men before she had to cope with someone like Damon...but she'd never wanted to practise her wiles on anyone before she'd met Damon.

This was entirely his fault. If he hadn't been so sexy and gorgeous she'd never have fallen in love with him and she wouldn't be in this humiliating position now.

'Kat, come out of there...please?' he said in his most coaxing voice.

She'd heard him use just that tone on their patients sometimes and she'd wondered how persuasive it would be if he ever turned it on her.

Now she knew.

'Why?' she demanded grumpily, knowing full well that she was eventually going to do what he asked. How could she refuse him when just the sound of his voice was sending her into meltdown?

'Because I want to see your face when I tell you how flattering that is.'

'Flattering?' she repeated suspiciously, still not ready to relinquish her hold on her camouflage.

'Wouldn't you be flattered if I'd just told you I'd spent an hour and a half bathing, shaving, washing my hair and—'

'And painting your toenails?' she prompted, sliding one foot across the bed until it reached the edge of the covers then wiggling her toes at him. There was no point in trying to stay cross and crabby when she knew that she was bound to succumb to his charm.

'Well, I'm not certain that I'd be willing to go quite that far,' he hedged with a chuckle, 'but I'm still very flattered that you did.'

'Really?' She pulled the covers down just far enough to peer over them.

'Really. *And* I'm sorry I upset you by taking so long last night.'

'How sorry?' she asked, suddenly fixing him with an intent gaze.

His expression turned wary. 'What do you mean?'

'How sorry are you that you took so long last night?' she clarified, suddenly nervous about what she was going to suggest. 'Sorry enough to take me out for a meal, perhaps?'

'Well, I don't know when we're both going to have an evening free together,' he said, sidestepping a direct answer.

'But, in principle, you'll agree that you owe me a meal the first time we're both free?'

She crossed her fingers while she waited for his reply. It was obvious that she wasn't going to get anywhere with her attempts at courting him if he always had excuses not to spend time with her.

At home, he always seemed be busy with his work

or sorting through his brother's things. She was beginning to suspect that he could probably stretch that chore out until all the formalities over the will had been finalised and the reason for their marriage gone.

If they went out for a meal together, he would have no excuse not to concentrate on just the two of them.

'OK,' he conceded. 'I agree that I owe you a meal the first evening we're both free.'

'And another meal each time you come to bed after I've fallen asleep?' she added cheekily.

'Woman, you'd bankrupt me,' he exclaimed with a laugh, and rolled away to sit up on the edge of the bed.

She'd been quite disappointed to see that he was wearing a pair of silky navy boxer shorts when he strode out of the room, apparently completely unaffected by the thought that she was watching him.

'Sister Gill—Cade,' called a voice, and Katherine was smiling when she turned. At least it was taking everybody else just as long to get used to her change of name.

It was Fran over by the office, beckoning her.

'Problem, Fran?' she asked when she joined her.

'That depends what you mean by a problem,' her friend temporised. 'I'm hoping you'll be able to do me a favour.'

Katherine groaned silently. At a guess, Fran was going to want to swap shifts again, and it had taken ages for her to be able to pin Damon down to an evening for their promised meal.

'What's the favour? Change shifts?'

When she'd been single she hadn't really minded what shifts she worked, so she'd been the one everyone had come to when work had clashed with private lives.

Unfortunately, her availability didn't seem to have changed much with her marriage. If anything, it seemed as if Damon was working even longer hours than before, so it didn't matter what shift changes she agreed to.

She'd made a joke of the fact that it was purely to save his pocket that he now managed to avoid coming to bed after she'd fallen asleep. Even so, it seemed as if his head hardly touched the pillow before he was gone, so it didn't make a great deal of difference.

Nearly a week had gone by and they still hadn't been out for their meal because their shifts just hadn't matched up till now. He would be late again tonight and she was on late tomorrow, but with any luck they would actually both be free the night after that—but she wouldn't put it past him to take on extra work just so that he could maintain his comfort zone between them.

'I'm supposed to be on late today,' Fran began in her best wheedling tone. 'Now Dave has been asked if he'll do a swap for a colleague with a sick child. Of course he said yes, but we were going to go out for a special meal together.'

'Special?' Katherine questioned, her antennae picking something up in her friend's voice.

'If you do a long day today to cover for the second part of my shift, I'll tell you about it,' Fran said tantalisingly.

'Am I allowed to guess?' Katherine teased in return, knowing already that she was going to agree. She'd done some quick mental calculations. If she did this swap with Fran, it would mean that she and Damon were both free tomorrow night, a whole twenty-four hours earlier than she'd expected. It would leave him far less time to manufacture excuses why they couldn't go.

Perhaps then she'd be able to start to persuade him to let go of his aversion to a closer relationship.

'If you'll agree, you can guess as many times as you like,' Fran promised.

'Well, then, I've only got one question—has he already bought the ring?'

Fran gave a squeal and had to cover her mouth quickly.

'How did you guess?' she demanded crossly. 'We were going to make an announcement tomorrow.'

'I can keep a secret,' Katherine promised. She'd had enough practice over the last few weeks, she thought wryly. Fran would probably never believe her if she told her the truth about her marriage to Damon. 'And as for how I know, I've always thought the two of you made a good couple, right from the first time you went out with him.'

'I think so, too, but thank you for saying it,' Fran said rather smugly, obviously over the moon with excitement. 'So, will you do it?'

'On condition that you'll do my late tomorrow,' Katherine bargained, and the deal was struck.

It was a long, hard shift but with the prospect of her promised meal with Damon coming one day closer it went by fairly easily.

Paolo Serapiglia had left them yesterday, his most recent crisis resolved by the extra blood transfusion. It would have been nice if they'd been able to say goodbye to him knowing that he wasn't going to have to come back again, but he was already booked in for his next transfusion in ten days' time. Hopefully, he was back on track for his usual three-times-a-month routine—unless he forgot his limitations and went chasing the pretty girls again.

Ian Longrigg had gone home, too, but in his case, as with any asthmatic, there was no way of knowing when he might appear again. It could be tomorrow but it could be next month or even next year.

His parents had gone away with some information on a variation of some Russian breathing exercises, and there was a possibility that the whole family might be moving to a new house fairly soon.

'It's still within the hospital's catchment area but it's out of the town,' Mrs Longrigg had told Katherine. 'Someone did a conversion of a barn but luckily didn't put in all the modern fitted carpets and suchlike that seem to trigger asthma in many people. We had a word with a vet your husband put us in contact with—an asthma sufferer like Ian—and he was able to give us all sorts of information and hints.'

She smiled at Katherine. 'We're just so grateful to Dr Cade for giving us the vet's name. He said that he found that he could cope with fur and feathers as long as he didn't also have to deal with the house mites that breed in centrally heated houses. This move could be a really important step in the right direction for Ian.'

'You mean the vet was able to choose to go into large animal farming rather than a city practice?' Katherine felt guilty that she hadn't followed up on the situation, especially as it had been her suggestion that Ian speak to Damon.

'He also does some exotic animals at one of the private zoos, and that's something Ian hadn't even thought of. If it was mostly outdoors work, that would suit him perfectly.'

Only time would tell how things worked out for the

youngster but she would certainly be crossing her fingers that he reached his goal.

'Goal!' cheered a voice, echoing her own thoughts, and she turned round just in time to see Frank swinging across the ward on his crutches in pursuit of a ball of tightly wadded paper.

'Frank!' she called sharply, and stopped him in his tracks. 'What on earth do you think you're doing?' she demanded as she strode angrily towards him.

'It was only sort of a game of football, but it's made out of paper so it won't do any harm.'

'The paper might not do any harm, but you great lumbering hulks could,' she pointed out, glaring at the other culprits. 'We've got someone here on traction, we've got another one feeling very sick on chemotherapy and at least two others who are still recovering from a trip to surgery. Any one of them could be disturbed or even injured by your horseplay.'

When she was certain she had his total attention she gestured towards the scaffolding holding the broken parts of his lower leg together.

'And what about you?' she demanded. 'How will you feel about your little game if you fall and shatter the bones where the pins go through? You know as well as I do what sort of problems you've already had with your leg. What if you damaged the repair job so badly that you had to have your leg amputated?'

'Amputated?' he repeated, visibly going quite green. 'That means cutting it off, doesn't it?'

'Yes, it does,' she confirmed crisply. 'Now, can you tell me how many first division football clubs employ players with artificial legs?'

She saw the horror in his face at the deliberately brutal picture she was painting and for a moment she felt quite guilty for frightening him. The trouble was, he'd been in such pain and off his feet for so long that now he was like an over-wound spring. He desperately needed to burn off some of his excess energy, but not at the expense of the recovery of his lower leg.

Katherine was frustrated because she didn't know what the answer was and the ward was very subdued for the next hour. Everyone had heard her reading Frank the riot act and it seemed to have put a real damper on the whole atmosphere.

'What's happened in here?' Damon demanded when he came in a little while after the event. 'It's almost as if someone's died, and I know that's not true.'

She told him about Frank's impromptu world cup among the beds and he raised his eyes to the ceiling.

'It would be far easier if the wards were run the same way as in the old days,' he muttered. 'Then the patients sat quietly and neatly in their beds and did what their doctors told them.'

Katherine chuckled. 'Yes, sometimes when we look back to compare that system with ours we're not quite sure whether they were the bad old days or the good old days. The trouble is,' she added more seriously, 'apart from his leg, he's disgustingly healthy, and at his age that's a recipe for disaster. Too much energy and not enough to do.'

'How about extra physio?' Damon suggested. 'That would take the springs out of his knees.'

'He's already having a session every morning, but...' She paused as a glimmer of an idea began to grow brighter. 'If it were to be packaged as body-building, I bet you'd get him interested.'

Damon grinned and her heart performed a double somersault before it started beating normally again.

'Clever girl!' he said. 'Kat, I think you've cracked it. How about if I have a word with the physio department and see what we can devise?'

Katherine was still glowing long after he'd left the ward on his way to look at an accident victim down in the casualty department. And she hadn't even thought to tell him about her rearranged shifts or the fact that they would now both be free to go out together tomorrow evening.

She had to console herself with a visit to the other half of the ward where, to make room for a set of twins injured in a car crash, Laurel Kent and Sally Cronin had ended up in adjacent beds.

Initially they'd seemed rather wary of each other, each old enough to pick up the clues that they were very obviously from different ends of the socioeconomic scale. It had only taken a glance at their almost identical tastes in music for the conversation to start. Now it had become quite a problem to get them to stop talking long enough to go to sleep.

'May I interrupt, ladies?' she asked as she perched on the side of one bed, and they both giggled.

'What's the latest report on your mother, Laurel? Has she finally got over being squeamish?'

'She's getting better,' Laurel said. 'She can do the cleaning of the yucky wounds where the wires go into my leg, but she still hates using the tool to turn the screws. She says she's afraid she's going to slip and break something, but I know that's not true. It's because she knows it's going to make my legs ache like toothache and she hates hurting me.'

'Her mum stops when Laurel pulls a face, so I have to make the faces for her,' her neighbour piped up. 'Her mum's not looking at me so I can screw my eyes up and open my mouth wide as if I'm screaming for Laurel.'

The two of them giggled again, as easy with each other as if their conspiracies had been going on for years rather than days.

She could hardly believe how different Sally Cronin looked already.

Now that most of the fear and pain had gone she'd lost that desperate look. It would be a while before her hair grew back and she still had an awful lot of healing to do where the burns had gone deepest, but it had been a relief all round when the plastic surgeon had decided there would be no need for surgical intervention.

Several days of regular meals had also had an almost miraculous effect on her. Where she'd come into the ward looking as though her bones were sharp enough to cut, she was now visibly beginning to gain some healthy weight.

'Hey, Sister, I went to visit my gran again today,' she announced cheerfully. 'She was sitting out of her bed in a chair. Her doctor says we'll probably be ready to go home at the same time. That's good isn't it?'

'Wonderful,' she agreed, especially knowing just how close the two of them had come to dying. The only thing Katherine hadn't been able to find out was where the two of them would be going when they were ready to leave the hospital.

She didn't mention this to Sally—it would only give her something to worry about and might even slow down her recovery—but even the television and news-paper coverage of the near-tragedy had mentioned the fact that the house would never be habitable again.

Perhaps Damon could find out what was happening.

She would have to remember to ask him…as well as telling him about their revised dinner date.

'This was downright sneaky,' Damon complained when the waiter finally left them to peruse the menus.

'Sneaky? Why? You did promise to take me out for a meal the next time we were both off duty together.' She gave him a triumphant smile and went back to looking at the long list of sumptuous dishes.

Well, it was either that or she'd be spending the evening gazing at Damon. He certainly looked good enough to eat and it was purely coincidental that the shirt he'd chosen to wear almost exactly matched her favourite blue dress.

It took a whole glass of wine and over half an hour before Damon finally allowed himself to relax, but from then on the evening was wonderful.

It was almost as if they'd gone back to the days before she'd begged him to marry her, when they'd been good friends who could talk about almost anything to each other.

The food was probably wonderful, too, but Katherine didn't really care what she was eating. What mattered to her was that she and the man she loved were actually talking to each other again.

Gradually, over the course of the evening, Damon had even started touching her the way he used to, a fleeting contact between their fingers when he steadied her glass to refill it, a soft press of his hand over hers to emphasise a point in their conversation.

He was also laughing again, his head thrown back in open enjoyment of her tales of the happenings on Windermere Ward, while his eyes gleamed and glittered with the reflection of the candle flames.

His hands lingered on her shoulders when he helped her into her coat at the end of their evening and his fingers almost seemed to caress the back of her neck when he released the hair trapped under her collar.

'Shall we get a taxi or would you like to walk?' he offered, and her heart leapt at the thought that he, too, might be enjoying their evening too much to want it to end so soon.

'As long as it's not raining, I'd love to walk,' she said, her smile spilling over from the happiness filling her inside.

In her high heels she was only a few inches shorter than he was and they fitted together perfectly when he wrapped an arm around her shoulders and pulled her close to his side to match their paces.

Katherine was glowing by the time Damon opened the front door and ushered her into the flat, happier than she'd ever been before. It felt almost automatic for her to turn towards him in expectation of the kiss that would signal the end of one part of the evening and the start of the rest.

'Let me help you off with your coat,' he offered, and she stood quietly, almost humming with anticipation as he slid it off her shoulders and hung it away neatly.

'You'd probably like to use the bathroom first,' he suggested. 'Give me a shout when you've finished.'

Katherine wasn't certain whether the idea of a lengthy build-up to the big moment was quite what she wanted. It would probably have been easier on her nerves if he'd just taken her in his arms there and then, rather than waiting until the two of them were in bed.

Still, she was certainly no expert in these things, and if she was going to cram the same hour and a half's pampering she'd done the other night into just a few minutes, she'd better get on with it.

She was quick but Damon was faster.

It seemed as if she'd barely slid under the covers before he was climbing in on the other side of the bed.

Shyness overtook her suddenly, and she was lying stiffly on her back, waiting for Damon to make the first advance, when she felt his hand creep across the no man's land between them and capture her hand.

She held her breath as he threaded his fingers through hers then brought their joined hands up to his mouth for a gentle kiss on each knuckle.

'Kat, thank you for tonight,' he murmured, his voice husky in the softly lit room. 'I don't think I've ever enjoyed an evening more.'

CHAPTER NINE

KATHERINE smiled and felt as if she should almost be visibly glowing with the happy warmth that flooded through her.

It had been worth the risk after all. She'd been worried that Damon wouldn't like the way she'd reorganised their outing without consulting him, but it had turned out perfectly.

She didn't think they'd ever been closer than on their walk home...until now, lying side by side in the centre of the bed.

She gave his hand a squeeze, worried that he might be waiting for her response to his gentle overture before he embarked on the irrevocable step of consummating their marriage.

'Damon?' she murmured when he still lay silently beside her. Her heart was performing an uneven polka at the thought that he might want her to take the initiative. Was she going to have to tell him in words of one syllable that she was almost a complete novice?

Finally, the suspense was too much. What was he waiting for?

Absolutely nothing, she discovered when she dared to peep at him.

While she'd been lying there, weaving fantasies about the real start to their marriage, he'd been falling asleep!

For a moment she contemplated giving him a shake to wake him up but the shadows under his eyes had been darkening visibly by the day and she couldn't make herself do it.

Instead of going out for a meal, he would probably have benefited more from an early night, but much as she regretted the premature end to the evening, she couldn't bring herself to regret spending the time together.

She watched him a little longer, enjoying the freedom to examine the slightly asymmetrical curves of his eyebrows and the straight blade of his nose. His mouth was something she'd fantasised about for two years, and the handful of kisses she'd finally shared with him had only made the fantasies more vivid.

The more she thought about the situation, the more she realised that persuading Damon to marry her was the best thing she'd ever done. Oh, she might be the only one in love at the moment, but once he'd relaxed this evening she'd caught glimpses of his own high regard for her and had every confidence that it would grow.

One of these days, if everything worked out well, she hoped she'd be able to thank her grandmother for indirectly giving her the idea to propose. If she hadn't been talking about leap year traditions, Katherine would never have come up with marriage as a solution to the nightmare she'd overheard.

In the meantime, everything was still a bit of a mess but, as her grandmother would say, she'd made her bed and now she was having to lie in it…even if she would rather be rolling about in it, making mad, passionate love.

Anyway, she wasn't going to meekly put up with the status quo. The success of their evening had only made her more determined to show Damon that what they had could be nurtured into a relationship to last a life-time. All she had to do was work out ways to combine old-fashioned courtship with sizzling seduction and he wouldn't be able to resist.

She closed her eyes to concentrate on possible scenarios and her mouth was still curved in a wicked smile when sleep overtook her.

When her breathing slowed and her hand finally grew limp in his grasp Damon stealthily turned to face the woman sleeping beside him.

It had taken every ounce of self-control he possessed to lie there and pretend to go to sleep, knowing that Kat wanted him to kiss her.

He'd wanted it too, had wanted more than that from the moment he'd seen her standing there in that blue dress.

She'd worn it a couple of times before to staff dos, and every time he saw the way the supple fabric outlined the slender perfection of her body all he could think about was taking it off to sample that body.

He'd been convinced that the evening would be a disaster, with his mind obsessively following its own track, but within half an hour they'd seemed to have rediscovered their own special rapport again.

Kat had made him laugh aloud with her stories and he'd enjoyed himself so much that he hadn't wanted the evening to end. Unfortunately, the walk home had obviously led Kat's thoughts along the same hopeful track as his.

It had nearly killed him to take her coat off and suggest she get ready for bed when the soft pout of her lips had told him what she had really wanted him to do. Only his decision to fake sleep had saved him from groaning aloud when he'd seen her waiting for him, the covers pulled demurely up to her chin.

Dammit, he wished he hadn't given her his word. What on earth had made him think that he'd be able to go to bed with her day after day for however long it took for her grandmother's home to be safe? If he didn't go stark raving mad with thwarted desire he'd deserve a solid gold medal for fortitude.

'Whatever doesn't kill you makes you strong,' he whispered, hoping the repetition would help him fight the attraction.

Unfortunately, Kat's silky hair was spread across the plain white pillow like a river of dark honey just waiting for the stroke of his fingers. Her sleep-softened lips were begging for the touch of his, a siren's lure that seriously undermined his resolve. It was almost unbelievable that this woman he'd married was unaware of exactly how unconsciously sexy she was.

He daren't allow his eyes to stray over the lacy top of that damned revealing nightdress but he couldn't stop his mind from imagining just how tempting she would look without it.

He clenched his hands into white-knuckled fists and closed his eyes while he took a couple of slow, deep breaths.

'Whatever doesn't kill you makes you strong,' he repeated fiercely. There was no point in praying for deliverance from this torment because it could be months before the resolution of her family's legal problems would release him from his promise.

All he could do was pray for sleep to come… quickly.

'Welcome, my dears,' Katherine's grandmother said with a wide smile as she held the front door open. 'I'm so glad the two of you were able to visit.'

Katherine immediately felt guilty. She and Damon had been putting her family off for several weeks now, and although neither of them had said anything she knew it was because they weren't absolutely certain that she would be able to fool the people who knew her best.

There was no problem at the hospital. Everyone saw exactly what they wanted to see—a happy newly married couple who'd always got on well with each other.

There was absolutely no tension between them at work because overt displays of passion or even affection would have been out of place. They had continued to work together as though nothing had changed.

It was going to be a different matter over the next couple of days.

It had been bad enough knowing that her mother and grandmother were watching them like hawks in the run up to the wedding, and worse still trying to act like honeymooners in front of the two of them when she and Damon were little more than friends.

This time there was the additional handicap of a build-up of several weeks of tension between them. Katherine had been trying to find ways to foster intimacy between them while Damon seemed intent on maintaining a friendly distance.

She was sitting watching Damon effortlessly charming her grandmother while she sat on the other side of the room with her mother. There was an unwanted cup of tea cradled in her hand and she was supposed to be examining the nearly finished piece of tapestry her mother was doing, but she couldn't stop her eyes from straying over to Damon.

Suddenly she realised that she was looking at this visit in entirely the wrong way.

She shouldn't be sitting here worrying whether her family would be able to spot the cracks in the façade of the marriage. Katherine realised with a growing feeling of excitement that what she should be doing was taking full advantage of the situation while leaving Damon no way to object.

A series of scenes began to play in her head and she had to work hard not to grin at her own deviousness.

Her first chance to put her plan into action came only minutes later when her grandmother started to show Damon an album of family photos.

'Come over here, Katherine.' A slender veined hand beckoned imperiously. 'Have you seen these since I reorganised them all into new albums?'

She willingly put her cup aside and hurried over to join them. She could have hugged her grandmother for providing her with an ideal opportunity so quickly.

When Damon would have moved aside on the settee to allow her room to sit, she forestalled him by settling herself right on his lap.

'Now we can all see,' she said brightly, reaching for the album and laying it across her lap.

She was very aware of the tension holding Damon rigid underneath her. His muscles were so tight that he was almost vibrating and suddenly she had second thoughts about subjecting him to this. If he really disliked having her this close she was making a big mistake.

'Am I too heavy for you?' she asked, grabbing the first excuse she could think of to get out of the situation she'd engineered.

She'd started to slide off his knees when he wrapped an arm around her waist and pulled her back.

'Not at all,' he said easily, sounding far more relaxed than she did about it. Much to her surprise he even left his arm wrapped around her waist.

While she turned the pages her grandmother kept up a running commentary about the various members of the family grouped in each picture, but Katherine's brain was worrying at the phenomenon of Damon's easy capitulation.

It was several minutes before she realised that, although she'd just taken their public intimacy to a new level in front of her family, his acceptance didn't necessarily signal a breakthrough in their real relationship. All it meant was that Damon was good at playing along with her in front of her family, just the way she'd anticipated.

That thought made her want to be a little bolder but it took her several minutes to come up with another apparently spontaneous move.

Next time he leant forward to look closer at one of the photos she looped her free arm around his shoulders, as though needing the contact for balance. When he sat up again her hand brushed across the back of his neck as if by accident, coming to rest with her fingers buried in the silky hair on the back of his head.

Suddenly the tension was back and the contact between them was heightened when he turned his head to gaze directly into her waiting eyes for several silent seconds.

It was almost as if he was trying to ask her what she was up to.

She thought she'd managed to successfully maintain her air of innocence when he slowly looked away again, but then his hand began to move at her waist, his thumb coming to rest just beneath the swell of her breast.

Katherine froze, wondering exactly how far he was going to go, but he remained motionless.

Almost unconsciously she flexed her fingers in the silky strands of his hair, and as if one movement had caused the other his fingers moved again, ending up even closer to her vulnerable curves.

He turned his head and looked at her again and this time she saw the unmistakable light of challenge in his eyes.

As if she'd been jolted by an electric shock, her heart stumbled then began to race when she felt a tightening sensation as her breasts signalled her burgeoning arousal.

With his hand where it was, there was no way he could miss her body's reactions to his touch and she knew he'd taken note when one corner of his mouth lifted in the start of a grin.

'Are you two listening to me?' her grandmother demanded suddenly, jerking both of them out of their preoccupation with their silent byplay.

'Give them a chance, Beatrice,' her mother said from the other side of the room, her tapestry abandoned on her lap. 'They've only been married a short while. They're bound to be much more interested in each other than a book full of old photographs. They wouldn't be normal otherwise.'

Katherine felt her cheeks growing warm, and when she heard Damon's chuckle at her mixture of guilt and embarrassment she could have hit him.

The whole idea was for her to be in control of the situation so that she could direct what was happening.

Instead, she'd become so involved in the sensations that poured through her when he touched her that she'd completely lost her focus.

Unfortunately, in spite of her determination, the same thing seemed to happen each time she initiated some apparently casual intimacy—her hand resting on his shoulder when she reached across him to put a plate on the table, her body brushing against his as she passed him in a doorway.

At first Damon had stiffened in surprise at what she was doing, but then he would retaliate in kind and she was lost.

'It's because I'm in love with him,' she muttered under her breath when she'd just lost another round of their silent battle.

She'd offered their services to do the washing-up so that she would be able to stand close enough to torment him with 'accidental' brushes of her body. She had ended up pinned against the front of a cupboard by the whole virile length of him while he 'innocently' reached over her to put the cups away.

'It's all right for him,' she muttered crossly. 'He manages to keep a clear head no matter what I do because he's not emotionally involved in what he's doing to me.'

Still, she had to admit that she was enjoying herself whether she was winning or not. In the last couple of hours she'd been hugged and tickled and kissed and had loved every minute of it—as had her watching family.

One thing that worried her was how she was going to explain what she was doing when they were finally alone in their room. She didn't think she'd be able to keep her face straight if she tried to claim that it was only intended to convince her family.

What if Damon had realised that she had her own secret agenda? She'd been trying for a measure of subtlety, so it was unlikely that he would guess she was trying to make him fall in love with her.

What if he thought she was actually trying to signal her willingness to extend their agreement to include intimacy, while still intending to terminate it when the legalities were finalised?

She nearly panicked at the thought and found herself watching him closely for clues. Gradually, she became more and more convinced that he was actually responding to her advances with genuine interest.

Did this mean that he was beginning to care too? That he wanted more than their paper agreement?

'Sorry if I wasn't very quick on the uptake,' Damon said as soon as he closed the bedroom door behind them that night. 'I didn't realise what was going on at first.'

Katherine was wary. She needed to know exactly what he meant before she made a fool of herself.

'You should have told me that you were worried,' he continued cheerfully as he began to unbutton his shirt, apparently completely unaware that she was watching. 'I hope I've been playing my part all right.'

'Playing your part?' she said numbly, her pleasure in his naked chest destroyed by the horrible premonition tightening its claws around her heart.

'Well, you're trying to make certain your family believe the marriage is real so they'll let us know when the will's been sorted out, aren't you?'

She forced a smile to her face when she felt more

like crying with disappointment. 'Well, it's not as if it's something we can ask them directly,' she pointed out quietly, while her heart bled for yet another dashed hope.

She'd honestly believed that he was enjoying their games and relishing the physical contact as much as she was. It was such a blow to find out that while she'd been celebrating the success of her scheme to draw them closer to each other, he'd only been pretending for the sake of their audience.

The worst part about the whole situation was that she had no one to talk to about her heartache. For nearly two years he had been her best friend and confidant, and now, when she needed his listening ear most, he was the last person she could confide in.

In contrast to the laughter and high spirits that had filled the evening, she could find almost nothing to say as they prepared for bed.

She knew Damon was watching her and she dreaded having to find answers were he to ask her what was wrong, but he also seemed preoccupied.

She turned straight onto her side under the covers and curled up into a defensive ball, convinced that the bed had grown wider since they'd last shared it. Even so, she was very aware of the way the heat from his body reached her across the acres of mattress separating them.

'Goodnight,' she heard him whisper before he grew still and his breathing deepened into a pattern that told her he slept.

Only then did she allow her silent tears to fall.

A sharp rap on the door woke the two of them up the next morning, and a quick glance at the forgotten alarm clock told Katherine that it was several hours after they normally got up.

'Are you two decent?' her mother called from outside the door. 'I've brought you breakfast in bed as a treat.'

Damon shot up in the bed and reached for the robe draped across the foot to make himself presentable before he called for her mother to come in.

Katherine dragged her fingers through her tangled hair and rubbed her hands over her face, hoping that no one would be able to tell that she'd been crying. She could hardly blame anyone else for her heartache—she'd brought it on herself when she'd decided she didn't want to stick to her agreement with Damon.

It was little consolation to see that he looked as if he'd had as little sleep as she had, not when she knew he'd been totally oblivious to her misery in the night.

'You didn't have to do this,' Damon said as he helped her mother to settle the tray across his lap. 'It's a long way to carry an awkward load and we're perfectly capable of getting our own.'

'Well, Beatrice and I were beginning to wonder if you were going to sleep the morning away and we didn't want to disappear without letting you know where we're going.'

'You're going out?' Katherine heard how rusty her voice sounded and winced, hoping no one would comment. 'Have the two of you been invited out to lunch?'

'No, dear. Nothing like that. We've got an appointment with your grandfather's solicitor—something to do with his will.'

Katherine couldn't help the guilty flush that crept up her throat and into her face. Were they going to inform the man that she'd fulfilled the conditions? Would they come home in a couple of hours and tell them that everything had been finalised?

Part of her longed for the worry to be over, but the other part, including her heart, desperately wanted more time to spend with Damon.

'How long are you likely to be? Do you want me to cook lunch?'

'Oh, no, dear. We'll probably stop in town and have a meal. Sorry to desert you like this, but at least it will give you two some time to yourselves.'

Katherine wanted to object but her mother had turned and was already on her way to the door.

'If we're not back by the time you need to set off, just leave the porch light on and lock up. We'll have keys with us.'

She threw them a little wave and sailed blithely out of the door.

Katherine leant weakly back against the headboard and groaned.

'How can she do this to us?' she demanded as soon as her mother's footsteps had faded into the distance. 'If they stay out, we'll have to go back to the hospital without finding out what's going on. It could be weeks before we visit them again and how do we bring up the topic of my grandfather's will *then* without making them suspicious?'

Damon was quiet for a moment, staring at the contents of the tray without making any attempt at sampling any of it.

'Are you in that much of a hurry to end our agreement?' he asked quietly. 'I thought we were probably going to have to wait until at least midsummer so that the legal eagles didn't get suspicious.'

'Well, yes, but…we hardly want to stay trapped in

this situation any longer than necessary...do we?' She was so confused by his reaction that she'd been reduced to babbling. For a moment it had almost seemed as if he wasn't any keener for the parting of the ways to come than she was.

'Kat, I think we're just going to have to get used to it,' he said and reached for a warm, flaky croissant with admirable calm. 'It's not as if we've got other partners waiting in the wings and we've always been good friends. What does it matter if it takes a few weeks longer before we know the answer?'

Katherine nearly screamed that the uncertainty would kill her, but then her more rational side intervened just in time. She took a steadying breath and tried to cultivate a thoughtful expression.

'I suppose you're right,' she agreed. 'It's less expensive for both of us to share your flat than pay for separate accommodation. We've been friends for long enough to be able to live together fairly easily and, best of all, you're housebroken.'

'What?'

He sounded outraged by her pragmatic summing-up but she chose to take it another way.

'Well,' she continued light-heartedly, 'you don't mind doing your share of the cooking and washing-up, you leave the bathroom tidy and you don't snore.'

'Well, thank you very much for the glowing testimonial, Kat,' he grumbled. 'I'll be sure to ask you for a written reference when I need one.'

'You're welcome, Damon,' she said breezily, suddenly feeling much happier. Although why his fit of pique should have that effect on her she didn't know. 'Now, tell me, are you going to hog everything on that tray, because if so I might have to revise that testimonial?'

'Why have I had to come in the kiddies' ward?' demanded an angry voice as Katherine reported for duty the next morning.

The owner of the voice couldn't have been more than about thirteen or fourteen but her face was set in a world-weary expression more suited to a middle-aged woman.

Katherine sighed. She had a feeling that today was going to be one of *those* days.

She watched for a moment and confirmed that the junior nurse was having no difficulty in persuading her obstreperous charge to do as she was told. There would be time enough for her to find out what was going on.

'Morning, Lenny. Any disasters to report or is everything sweetness and light today?'

'Actually, I had a very peaceful night, thank you,' he said with a grin. 'But I think all that is about to change.'

He cocked his head towards the female side of the department to draw Katherine's attention to that same shrill voice.

'What's the story?' she demanded as she helped herself to a mug of coffee. She had a feeling she was going to need all the help she could get today.

'Bungled abortion, we suspect, but it's been impossible to get her to talk.'

'How much permanent damage?'

Katherine always dreaded encountering a repeat of a case she'd seen during her training—a fifteen-year-old who'd had to have a hysterectomy because of a badly perforated uterus. She'd been at the youngster's side when the surgeon had tried to explain that the operation had been necessary to save her life.

'It looks like she's been lucky—this time,' he said quietly. 'They were able to do a D and C and she's on ergometrine.'

'Why is she here instead of up on Obstetrics and Gynaecology?'

'No room,' he said succinctly. 'Anyway, at her age she really belongs down here.'

'She obviously doesn't agree,' Katherine said with chuckle as the argument carried on just out of sight. 'Perhaps you'd better get me up to speed on the rest of them and then I'll take a wander over and introduce myself.'

'Perhaps you'd better have a rabies shot first,' he advised with a twinkle then settled down to make his report.

'I've come to collect my daughter,' announced a smartly dressed gentleman about an hour later. 'Celia Lennard,' he added with a quick glance at his watch. 'Can we hurry it up a bit? I've got classes to teach this morning.'

Katherine blinked. 'Ah, Mr Lennard, have you spoken with Celia's doctor? I don't think she's ready to go home just yet.'

'Well, that's all right. You just get me one of those release forms and I'll sign it. Then you won't have to worry that we'll be suing the hospital.'

'That *wasn't* what I was worried about,' she said sharply. 'My concern is for Celia.'

And she *was* concerned about the child because that's what she was for all her pretence at maturity.

She was pretty in a delicate sort of way and would

probably always look younger than her age. At the moment, for all her bravado, she seemed like a very frightened little girl.

'Well, when I take her home you won't have to be concerned any more,' he said with a smug smile that instantly put Katherine's back up.

'If you'd like to take a seat in here for a minute,' she suggested, leading him towards the interview room. 'It's not strictly visiting time at the moment and there are technicians in the ward taking blood samples from the patients to go up to the labs, and dressings being changed on wounds.'

It wasn't true, but he obviously didn't know any better and sat himself in the little room without an argument. She'd had a feeling that he wouldn't want to wait around where he might see any of the more gruesome sights.

It only took a couple of minutes for Katherine to telephone a message through to Celia's surgeon and she was just putting the phone down when Damon arrived on the ward.

'Damon. Thank God you're here!' she breathed as she grabbed his arm and dragged him into the office. 'I need you to do me a favour.'

'Another one? What is it this time?' he teased, and waggled his eyebrows up and down.

'This is serious, Damon,' she said sternly and in a matter of moments had explained the situation to him.

'So what do you want me to do? Try to persuade him to leave his daughter here until tomorrow or the next day? You know that as she's a minor, legally he *can* sign a release and take her away. We'd have to have her made a ward of court to keep her here against his will.'

'I know that,' she said impatiently. 'And I might have got hold of completely the wrong end of the stick, but I've got a nasty feeling about this one.'

Damon reached for her hand and gave it a quick squeeze. 'Say no more. I'll go and spin him a few yards of flannel while you see what you can find out.'

To her surprise, he didn't just release her hand but lifted it up to his lips for a fleeting kiss.

CHAPTER TEN

KATHERINE was still curled up on top of the bed wrapped in Damon's robe when she heard him let himself into the flat that night.

'Kat? Where are you?' he called, and she tracked his approach, half welcoming and half dreading the moment he found her.

He paused in the doorway, silhouetted by the soft light from the sitting room, and she squeezed her eyes tight shut, waiting for him to switch this one on too...except he didn't.

'Prefer the dark?' he asked quietly as he approached the bed.

'If you don't mind,' she whispered, turning her head away from him. 'I'm not a pretty sight at the moment.'

He stood silently beside her for a moment before she felt the mattress dip under his weight.

'Would a hug from a friend help?' he offered, and she couldn't accept fast enough.

'Oh, Damon,' she sobbed as she surged up against his shoulder and wrapped frantic arms around his neck. 'I haven't been able to stop thinking about that poor girl.'

He soothed her silently, his arms wrapped securely around her as one hand stroked her back over and over again.

'I'm proud of you, you know,' he murmured into the near darkness. 'You had a feeling something wasn't right.'

171

'But I never imagined…' She shuddered. 'I was talking to her for nearly ten minutes and wasn't getting anywhere. Then I told her that her dad had come and was insisting that he wanted to take her home straight away.'

She remembered the way the child's smart-alec defiance had crumbled at the news. Suddenly she'd been nothing more than the frightened girl Katherine had suspected.

'He's *not* my dad, he's my stepfather,' she'd said through gritted teeth. 'And I hate him.'

'Celia,' Katherine had begun, but she'd got no further as the child began to sob.

'It's his fault,' she said accusingly, sounding much younger than her years. 'It's all his fault that I had to come here. He put the baby in me and then he made me get rid of it so Mum wouldn't find out what he's been doing to me.'

'She told me that he'd brought a large syringe home from the labs at the school where he teaches. He waited for her mother to go out to work then he filled it with salty water. Then he… Then he…' She shook her head, unable to continue.

'Shh, Kat, shh. It's all right,' Damon murmured, rocking her as if she were a frightened child herself. 'She's going to be all right.'

He hadn't known any more about the situation than she'd told him when she'd enlisted his help in keeping Mr Lennard out of the way for a while.

Finally the man had grown impatient at the delay and had insisted on being taken to see his daughter.

He must have suspected what had happened as soon as he saw Celia's tears. He'd tried to bluff his way out of it but when Celia had cowered away from him, refusing to leave the hospital until she spoke with her mother, he'd exploded with rage, trying to blame Kat for filling her head with lies.

Damon flexed the fingers of his right hand and winced. 'I'm proud of the way you wouldn't let him get near Celia, but I just wish I hadn't aimed for the bastard's chin,' he muttered gruffly, reliving the moment when he'd seen the man grab Kat to try to get her out of his way.

He nearly groaned aloud when he thought he'd set her crying again but then he realised that she was actually chuckling.

'My hero,' she teased him through her tears, and she turned in his arms to search for his injured hand. 'Is it badly bruised?'

'Worse than it would have been if I'd aimed for his stomach. Even his nose would have been a softer target,' he said in disgust, silently relishing the feel of gentle fingers stroking the swollen redness of his knuckles.

'Ah, but that might have made a mess on my clean floor,' she objected, then grew serious again. 'I'm just glad that the police were able to take him straight into custody. At least he won't be able to go near her again.'

Damon guided her head back to his shoulder and relished the opportunity to openly hold her in his arms. It was one thing to wait until she fell asleep each night so that he could lie close to her, but that almost seemed to increase his frustration.

He'd been watching for weeks now, waiting for Kat to say something…anything…to let him know that she wanted something more from their bogus marriage.

The worst part was knowing that it was his own fault. He'd backed himself into a corner when they'd

first met, when he'd still been reeling from the loss of
Damian, the last member of his family.

It was too late now to realise that his declaration that
he would never marry had probably been an obstinate
knee-jerk response to his unexpectedly strong reaction
to Kat.

He'd had two years to regret his hasty words so that
Kat's startling proposal had appeared in front of him
like a rope thrown to a drowning man. He'd been so
certain that once they were married proximity would
help her to realise that she didn't want it to end.

It hadn't happened as quickly as he'd anticipated but
he was still optimistic that it *would* happen. In fact,
he'd been pinning his hopes on the dream that she
would one day discover that she loved him.

When her mother and grandmother had gone off for
their appointment with the solicitor he'd been afraid
that he'd finally run out of time, but here they were,
still in limbo.

His thoughts were still following their well-worn
tracks when he finally realised that Kat had fallen
asleep in his arms.

He almost resented the fact that it was time to lay
her down but he knew she needed the sleep.

She seemed fragile and vulnerable as he lifted her
off his lap and settled her under the covers, still
wrapped in his robe. He gazed down at her for a long
moment and then, despite the pile of paperwork on his
desk waiting for attention, found himself stripping his
clothes off as he gave in to his need to be close to her.

It took no more than a minute before she was in his
arms again, this time with his body curved protectively
around her.

'Sleep well, Kat,' he whispered as he brushed a kiss over the top of her head. 'I love you.'

It was dark when Katherine woke but she had no idea what had brought her out of her sleep.

She turned her head awkwardly to peer at the bright green numbers on the alarm clock and saw that it was only a few minutes past midnight.

It took her several moments to realise that the reason why she was finding it difficult to move was because Damon had both arms wrapped around her.

She was also still wearing his thick towelling robe, and with Damon's additional heat she was nearly ready to melt.

Stealthily, she tried to slide away without waking him. If she was lucky she'd be able to exchange the robe for one of her thinner nighties and slide back into bed without Damon noticing.

'Where do you think you're going?' murmured a sleepy voice in her ear, and she froze, waiting for him to realise that he was holding her and release her to roll away to the other side of the bed.

The fact that he didn't make any attempt to move away completely scrambled her brain, but she was still far too hot.

'I'm…er… Your dressing gown's too hot and…and I was just going to take it off,'

'Allow me,' he said, and to her shock she felt him fumbling at her waist for the belt.

'Damon! What are you doing?' she demanded breathlessly, trying to hang onto the lapels to keep herself covered. After she'd nearly scrubbed herself raw to remove the taint of Mr Lennard's touch from her skin she hadn't bothered to do any more than pull

Damon's robe on. If he took it away she would be lying there naked.

'I'm helping you,' he said simply, and flicked both edges of the fabric out of her hands...then froze. 'Kat,' he said in a strangled voice. 'You aren't wearing anything underneath.'

'I—I know.' She gazed up at him, the planes and angles of his face starkly outlined by the forgotten light in the sitting room. He was looking down at her, his eyes travelling feverishly over what he had revealed and when she saw his fierce expression she was certain her heart would explode if it tried to beat any faster.

She knew she really ought to move away, or at least pull the robe over to cover herself again, but then he touched her breasts with gentle fingertips and she melted with a groan.

'Oh, Kat, your skin's so soft,' he whispered with a groan of his own as he began to explore.

By that time Katherine was beyond refusing him. Why should she when this was what she'd been wanting for more than two years?

It was bliss to lie there and revel in the touch of his hands and mouth but soon that wasn't enough. She needed to explore him too—to learn what the body she'd admired from a distance felt like when she could touch it all over.

'Kiss me,' Damon demanded huskily. 'Please, Kat, kiss me.'

He sounded almost afraid that she would refuse, but she couldn't when it was what she wanted, too.

Then one kiss wasn't enough. It led to more and wilder kissing and then touching until nothing would ever be enough until their bodies became one.

Katherine longed to tell him that she loved him, but

every time she found enough breath to speak the words he robbed her of it again with a fresh assault.

Finally she realised that she didn't really need words to tell him how she felt—her body could do it far better—and she gave him the gift of herself, body, heart and soul.

The first grey light of dawn was creeping round the edges of the curtains when Katherine woke to find herself wrapped once more in Damon's arms, this time with her head cradled on his shoulder.

She had no idea what time it was but when she tried to wriggle out of his grasp he wouldn't release her at all.

'Stay,' he whispered softly as he tightened his arms briefly, and she looked up in surprise to find him watching her.

She blushed when she saw the heated expression in his eyes and wished that he'd really meant it. There was nothing she would have liked better than for Damon to change his mind about their marriage. Unfortunately, she was old enough to realise that making love wasn't the same thing to a man as being in love.

Still, she couldn't find a trace of regret in her heart that their relationship had finally crossed the boundary between platonic and sexual. It would be hypocrisy if she did, after spending these short weeks trying to court him or even seduce him into doing just that.

There was a certain irony in the fact that it had happened when she'd least been prepared for it—no fancy perfume or lacy nightdress, just rough-dried hair and a tear-streaked face.

'Regrets, Kat?' Damon asked softly, and drew her

thoughts back to their present situation. He hooked a gentle knuckle under her chin and brought her gaze up to meet his. He had a slight frown pleating his forehead and she couldn't help wondering if his feelings about what had just happened between them were very different to hers.

'Do you?' she asked, taking the coward's way out by ducking a reply until she knew what he was thinking.

'Only that the night is over,' he said softly, and her heart gave an extra thump.

'Is it?' As soon as the words were out of her mouth she could hear how suggestive they could sound, but what she really wanted to know was whether that one night was all he wanted.

'There always comes a time to pay the piper,' he said soberly. 'You do realise that this means there can be no annulment of the marriage.'

Katherine's heart sank like a stone.

The last thing she'd expected him to talk about was the end of their marriage. When he'd talked about paying the piper her first thought had been that he'd realised they'd taken no precautions against pregnancy.

'Is that a problem?' she asked stiffly, wondering if he was going to resent the fact that it wouldn't be nearly so easy to end their marriage now it had been consummated.

The thought that she might already be carrying his child was too momentous to take in at the moment. She would have to concentrate on their immediate conversation before she let herself consider her options if she *had* conceived.

Suddenly Damon went up on one elbow so that he loomed over her in the shadowy light.

His chest looked impossibly broad and tantalisingly naked and her fingers longed to smooth their way across it, but it was the expression on his face that demanded her attention.

'No, Kat, it's not a problem for me,' he said, his voice growing heated. 'Dammit woman, I've been in love with you for months…long before we got married.'

'But…' she quavered, unable to believe what she was hearing. She shook her head and began again.

'But you said you had no intention of marrying,' she reminded him, her hands clenched into tight fists. 'It was one of the first conversations we ever had.'

'I know.' He sighed as he captured her fists and stroked them gently. Almost against her will, she felt herself softening. 'I honestly believed it at the time because it hadn't been long since I lost Damian.'

'You were hurting,' she whispered, remembering the look in his eyes and the way she'd wanted to make it go away. 'You'd lost so much and didn't want to chance losing any more.'

She'd understood the devastating forces that had made him come to such a decision. That was the only reason she'd been able to make herself accept the situation. It had only been his acceptance of her proposal of marriage that had made her think it was worth taking a chance. Not that her attempts at courtship had seemed to be very successful…

'That was before I realised you'd knocked me for six,' he continued suddenly, one finger stroking down the side of her cheek and along her jaw. 'Then I really found myself in a cleft stick. On one hand, I wanted to take the chance of telling you how I felt so that we could deepen our relationship into something permanent. On the other, I was seeing on a daily basis how much you loved your job and how good you were at it. I realised that you were a dedicated career woman so I resigned myself to working with you as a friend.'

Katherine was so amazed by his revelations that she didn't even think to correct his assumptions.

Yes, she loved her job, but she could never love it more than she loved him.

'Then we went to the Valentine's ball,' he continued with a wry smile at the memory. 'I knew you well enough to tell that you were worried about something, but I couldn't believe it when you proposed to me. It was like having a banquet handed to me on a plate.'

'It took you long enough to sample it,' she complained with a pout, at last daring to hint at her own feelings. 'I've been trying to court you for weeks.'

'Court me?' he said in amazement. 'Ha! And I thought you were just trying to drive me out of my mind. I've taken so many cold showers in the last few weeks that I nearly froze to death. And then I'd climb back into bed and take one look at you lying there and I might as well not have bothered torturing myself.'

'Oh, Damon, haven't we been idiots?' she said ruefully. 'If only we'd spent a little more time talking to each other, instead of making assumptions.'

'Idiots,' he agreed as he settled himself down beside her again and pulled the covers up over their shoulders. 'Still, we're both intelligent enough to learn from our mistakes.'

'You mean, we must make certain to talk more?' she suggested, although how she was supposed to concentrate on talking to the man when he was stroking his hand up and down her naked back she didn't know.

'We must make certain we let each other know what

we want and what our expectations are,' he added, his own voice beginning to have a distracted air.

'For example?' she prompted. 'What are your expectations of our marriage?'

'Oh, very modest. Just that it will be the longest and happiest one the world has ever known,' he said confidently. 'Well, I love you so much that it would just have to be,' he added softly.

The expression in his eyes was clear, even in the dim light, and she couldn't doubt what he was saying. Her heart seemed to swell with joy but there was one matter they hadn't covered.

'What about children?' she asked warily. 'We have to deal with them on a daily basis and—'

'And I'd love to have several of our own,' he confirmed easily. 'I loved having my siblings around and missed them terribly when they were gone.'

'How soon?' she persisted. 'Only I haven't checked the dates in my diary but we didn't take any precautions and—'

'As soon as you like,' he declared with a wicked grin. 'In fact, let's see if we can blister the bedroom paint some more while we try again.'

'Do you think they're going to be angry?' Katherine asked nervously as Damon drew up outside her grandmother's house.

Although their deception had turned out for the best, it was still preying on her mind.

Damon had finally dragged it out of her the other day and had insisted that they come down to visit to get rid of the guilt once and for all.

'If they are, it won't be for long,' he predicted. 'You

were only doing it to help your grandmother, so they'll have to take your good intentions into account.'

'I hope so,' she muttered as she let herself out of the car.

Their welcome was as warm as ever but Katherine was too tense to appreciate it. All she could think about was that her fraud might jeopardise her grandmother's ownership of the house she loved.

Damon must have realised how distracted she was and, knowing the reason, brought the conversation swiftly to the point.

'Beatrice, Kat and I have been living with a guilty secret for months now, and we need to get it off our chests,' he announced into the first lull.

'Oh, my dears,' her grandmother said, and Katherine saw her hands begin to tremble.

'We got married under false pretences,' he continued baldly. 'Kat overheard about her grandfather's will and begged me to marry her so that you wouldn't lose your home.'

The room was so silent Katherine could have heard a pin drop. It was almost as if they were all holding their breaths.

'She approached me because I was her closest male friend,' he continued steadily, 'and she proposed a platonic marriage that would be annulled as soon as we were sure the legalities were over.'

Katherine saw the stricken look that passed between her mother and her grandmother and felt worse than ever. She didn't dare look at Damon's face for fear she would start to cry. She should have been the one making the explanation, but he'd willingly taken on the onerous task when he'd realised how much the prospect filled her with trepidation.

'It's been preying on our minds that our fraud might cause you to lose your home after all, so we had to come and tell you.'

He stood silently, waiting for someone to speak, almost as if he were waiting for a firing squad.

'*Is* it a fraudulent marriage?' her grandmother demanded suddenly, her piercing gaze fixed on Katherine. 'You fulfilled all the requirements before your wedding day and you signed the register after the ceremony.'

'Well, yes, but…' Unhappily she found herself gazing down at the way her hands were twisting in her lap.

'Is it still a platonic marriage?'

Katherine's face flooded with scarlet at the blunt demand and couldn't answer.

'No. It's not,' Damon announced, coming to her rescue again.

'So you took advantage of the situation and helped yourself to my granddaughter,' Beatrice charged, stony-faced.

'No!' The unfairness of it had Katherine on her feet, hurrying over to wrap her arms around him. 'Damon didn't take advantage of me. I spent weeks trying to court him into making it a real marriage.'

'Well, thank goodness one of you found some gumption,' her grandmother snapped, obviously exasperated. 'Your mother and I began to despair that the two of you would ever come to your senses.'

'Beatrice!'

'Grandmother!'

The two outraged exclamations were almost simultaneous.

'Well,' she said defiantly, 'everyone else could see that the two of you loved each other. I was beginning to think that if I didn't do something to give you a push I'd be dead before I saw you married.'

Katherine had the strange feeling that the world had just turned upside down. This couldn't be her straight-as-an-arrow grandmother speaking, could it?

'Then I read that book all about the old superstitions—you know, leap year and Valentine's Day—and suddenly saw a way of—'

'You mean it was all a set-up?' Damon demanded suddenly, looking from one woman to the other. 'What about the will?'

It was her mother's turn to look guilty.

'I'm afraid that was my idea,' she admitted. 'I knew after my experiences with her grandfather that Katherine might just swallow the story.'

'You mean, you were never in danger of losing the house?'

When they both shook their heads Katherine didn't know whether to laugh or cry.

Damon didn't have any such doubts, suddenly bursting into full-throated chuckles.

'Oh, my God,' he said when they subsided enough to talk. 'I think I've changed my mind about having any children. Can you imagine what they'd turn out like with genes from this pair in their ancestry?'

'Grandchildren?' her mother said with a sudden gleam in her eyes.

'Great-grandchildren?' her grandmother said. 'When?'

'We'll let you know when we've decided,' Damon announced firmly as he began to usher Katherine towards the door. 'In the meantime, we've decided to take that honeymoon you disturbed—'

'Your mother got cold feet,' Beatrice said. 'She

wanted to spill the beans right then, but I pointed out that the two of you were already starting to want to cover up for each other. I persuaded her that you would be able to sort it out for yourselves—if we could get you sharing a room.'

'Beatrice!' her mother exclaimed, looking agitated. 'I think it's a case of least said, soonest mended. Let the two of them go off on their honeymoon. At least they won't be worrying about the roof over our heads.'

'And they might even start thinking about providing us with the next generation of...'

Their voices faded as Damon shut the front door firmly behind the two of them.

'How about it, Mrs Cade? Do you feel like catching up on some of the courtship we missed out on? I've discovered there's a very nice country house hotel not far from here where they serve meals by candlelight.'

'I think it sounds perfect. Very romantic. But we haven't brought any luggage with us.'

'That sounds even better to me,' he murmured with a wicked grin as he helped her into the car. 'A perfect way to continue our courtship.'

MILLS & BOON®

Makes any time special

Enjoy a romantic novel from Mills & Boon®

Presents...™   *Enchanted*™   TEMPTATION.

Historical Romance™   ◢MEDICAL ROMANCE™

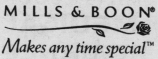

MILLS & BOON®

MEDICAL ROMANCE™

THE GIRL NEXT DOOR by Caroline Anderson
Audley Memorial Hospital

When surgeon Nick Sarazin and his two children, Ben and Amy, moved next door to ward sister Veronica Matthews, she helped as much as possible. It was clear to Ronnie that Nick had yet to let go of his wife's memory, and there'd only be heartache, loving this beautiful man...

THE MARRIAGE OF DR MARR by Lilian Darcy
Southshore # 3 of 4

Dr Julius Marr had been deeply impressed by Stephanie Reid's care of her mother, but afterwards he didn't know how to stay in touch—until he could offer her the job of receptionist at the practice. But until he'd tied up some loose ends, they couldn't move forward.

DR BRIGHT'S EXPECTATIONS by Abigail Gordon

Nurse Antonia Bliss first met paediatrician Jonathan Bright when she was dressed as the Easter Bunny! Was that why he thought she couldn't know her own mind? But his own expectations were so battered, he needed some excuse to keep her at a distance...

0002/\

Available from 3rd March 2000

Available at most branches of WH Smith, Tesco, Martins, Borders, Easons, Volume One/James Thin and most good paperback bookshops

MILLS & BOON®

MEDICAL
ROMANCE™

A SON FOR JOHN by Gill Sanderson
Bachelor Doctors

Since qualifying Dr John Cord had concentrated on work, trying to forget that he had loved and lost his Eleanor. But his new Obs and Gynae job brought her back into his life. Even more shocking was the sight of a photo on Ellie's desk of a young boy who was clearly his son!

IDYLLIC INTERLUDE by Helen Shelton

Surgeon Nathan Thomas borrowed his step-brother's Cornish cottage, only to find himself next door to a beautiful girl. Not one to poach, Nathan was horrified by his instant attraction to nurse Libby Deane, assuming she was Alistair's girlfriend.

AN ENTICING PROPOSAL by Meredith Webber

When nurse Paige Warren rescued a young Italian woman, she phoned Italy leaving a message for 'Marco', but Dr Marco Alberici—an Italian prince!—arrives in person, disrupting her surgery and her hormones! Should she really accept his invitation to return to Italy?

0002/03b

Available from 3rd March 2000

Available at most branches of WH Smith, Tesco, Martins, Borders, Easons, Volume One/James Thin and most good paperback bookshops

MILLS & BOON®

By Request™

Three bestselling romances brought back to you by popular demand

Latin Lovers

The Heat of Passion *by Lynne Graham*
Carlo vowed to bring Jessica to her knees,
however much she rejected him. But now she
faced a choice: three months in Carlo's bed, or
her father would go to jail.

The Right Choice *by Catherine George*
When Georgia arrived in Italy to teach English
to little Alessa, she was unprepared for her uncle,
the devastating Luca. Could she resist?

Vengeful Seduction *by Cathy Williams*
Lorenzo wanted revenge. Isobel had betrayed
him once—now she had to pay. But the tears
and pain of sacrifice had been price enough.
Now she wanted to win him back.

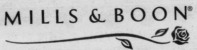